IN THIS COLLECTION

THE AWAKENING
After a rough night of partying, a young girl finds that she's changed and decides she's no longer going to allow herself to be a victim.

THE ORACLE BOARD
Bizarre things happen when a group of college freshmen get caught up using an oracle board during a Nor'Easter over a holiday weekend.

MABEL
A teenage boy finds a message from a girl who is in danger and needs help. But the place she lives at has been abandoned for years.

HEAR MORE
A priest fears for his life when he begins hearing demons. But only when he wears his newly acquired hearing aids.

KEYNOTE
The struggles of a peer at a weekend conference are mocked and ignored until the universe steps in.

DARK AWAKENINGS

A COLLECTION OF HAUNTING SHORT STORIES

RAY LECARA JR

SYNER-G PUBLISHING

SEATTLE

Published in the U.S. by Syner-G Publishing, Seattle.

Publisher's Cataloging-in-Publication Data
Names: LeCara, Ray Jr, author.
Title: *Dark Awakenings: A Collection of Haunting Short Stories* / Ray LeCara Jr.
Description: Seattle, WA: Syner-G Publishing, 2022. | Summary: Five stories about characters unexpectedly awakened to the darkness surrounding them. Those haunted places hidden in the shadows but always within the periphery. The places seldom talked about but very much feared.
Identifiers: LCCN: 2022918414 | ISBN: 978-1-7379394-5-0
Subjects: LCSH Short stories, American. | Nightmares--Fiction. | Good and evil--Fiction. | Horror. | BISAC FICTION / Short Stories (single author) | FICTION / Horror | FICTION / Thrillers / Supernatural
Classification: PS3612.E222 F76 2022 | DDC 813.6—dc23

Book Jacket Design © SGP | Front/Back Cover Image: RizalDeathrasher (Pixabay) | The Awakening image c/o Macaskill Wright | The Oracle Board images Dorothe (Pixabay)/George (Pixabay)/Châu Nguyễn (Pixabay) | Mable image c/o Mister Pittiager (Pixabay)/ Willfriend Wende (Pixabay)| Keynote image Yvette W (Pixabay) | Author image Gordon Johnson (Pixabay) | All other interior images licensed under Creative Commons Zero 1.0 Public Domain License

Printed in the USA | Syner-GPublishing.com

First Edition

To Josh

future filmmaker

"WE MAKE UP HORRORS TO HELP US
COPE WITH THE REAL ONES."
— STEPHEN KING

"EVERYBODY IS A BOOK OF BLOOD:
WHEREVER WE'RE OPENED.
WE'RE RED."
— CLIVE BARKER

"SOMETIMES IT IS RIGHT
TO FEAR THE DARK."
— PETER STRAUB

TABLE OF
CONTENTS

THE
AWAKENING

The beeping of the cell phone alarm did little to rouse Dez from bed. Nor did it help her throbbing temples. Awake for several minutes now, she was still groggy going over the events of the previous evening. Licking her dry lips, she slid the snooze button on the phone for the third time. Thank goodness today was Friday. Last night—a school night—was a late night. Luckily her parents didn't hear her come in. It wasn't like they even cared anyway.

Stretching herself out on the bed, Dez shielded her eyes from the invading rays of light making their way through the blinds. It was late May—springtime in New England. A time when the days were warming up while the nights remained cool. Though dressed in only a red tee and black booty shorts, she was uncomfortably warm.

Dez kicked back the dark sheets. Her skin was clammy. Sweaty. Something wasn't right. Thinking it might help ease the tension in her head, Dez extended her neck until it cracked. Nothing.

Rising, she looked at the stranger reflected before the dresser mirror. Her shoulder length ginger colored hair was strewn wildly about her freckled face. Thick reddish-brown eyebrows, badly in need of trimming, sat above bright green eyes outlined with black liner. Three piercings adorned her face: an eyebrow loop, a stud in her nostril, and another loop in her bottom lip. How she wished her nose were a little smaller and her lips a little fuller. She winced as she unconsciously bit her bottom lip hoping it'd swell.

Drawing herself closer to her reflection, she pulled back her hair to examine the hideous hickey on her neck. The kids at school will have a ball with this, she thought to herself. Showing up with a beauty mark this big was sure enough to attract unwelcome attention from the teachers, the counselors, and the freaks who always gossiped about her. And heaven forbid they should find out the boy she was with last night was in his twenties. She'd never hear the end of it.

Her gaze shifted from the reflection of herself to the items in her room. Such stuff seemed alien to her. It was as if the contents filling her room—the certificates and trophies with her name on them—belonged to another person.

Academic accolades and gymnastic trophies all bore her full name. A name she hated: Desdemona Paine. Desdemona Zora Paine. Once a strong student when school interested her and when life at home was better, things had changed over the last few years.

Reminders of the past triggered her. Already having worked her way through the porcelain dolls her grandmother bought her when she was a child, giving them darker clothes and drawing in raccoon eyes with permanent marker, she wondered why so much of the other stuff was still up on her walls. Why hadn't she thrown the stuff away yet? She spent very little time at home these days anyway.

Stepping into the adjoining bathroom, Dez hoped a shower would clear her thoughts and ease the pain in her head. But the water from the showerhead pelted her skin like tiny barbs. Cold or hot, it did nothing to soothe the young girl's malaise. She felt drained. Fatigued. Lethargic.

"Well, you were out late," she whispered to herself while running her hands through her long hair to draw out the kinks. And it wasn't the first time she snuck out to stay up all night.

Lifting her face to meet the shower spray, Dez reduced the cold water. She let the scalding water turn her pale skin red in an attempt to wash off the growing unease of the previous evening. In pieces, thoughts of the encounter came back leaving her feeling vulnerable. She was not proud of her lack of restraint or her lack of judgment. Meeting up with the hot boy she met on Tinder was an impetuous, if not rebellious, act. But it was difficult to say no. He was mesmerizing. Seductive. He clearly knew what he wanted. Knew all the right words to say. She couldn't resist him. It made her reckless.

Slowly, with the rising steam, the realization of the prior night worked its way up her throat. She had the queer feeling of things out of place. Of something amiss and not quite right.

She felt exposed. Used, even. No longer able to hold it back, her knees buckled. Her entire body convulsed in a fit of sobs.

It was then, at her weakest moment, that the shower curtain was violently jerked aside.

"Out all night, were you?" her drunken stepfather charged.

Startled, Dez let out a cry as she attempted to shield her naked body.

Not the first time he invaded her privacy while in the bathroom, he had developed a habit of barging in whenever he felt like it. His actions had become more brazen since he married her mother, especially if she was at work like today. It wasn't even his bathroom. Her parents had their own private one attached to their bedroom.

No, he now acted as if he had a right to her. Especially since there were no locks on the doors to dissuade him. But Dez would have none of it. If her mom wouldn't say anything, Dez certainly would. After all, it was her right. Her privacy. It was her body.

Dressed only in stained white underwear, her stepfather's grotesquely overweight hairy body repulsed her. She hated the way he looked, the way he smelled. She hated the way he carried himself. Everything about him disgusted her so much she wished him dead and hated her mother for marrying him.

Dez cowered from her stepfather's touch as he grabbed for her.

Then he saw the hickey.

"I always knew you were trouble. Damn whore. From the moment I met you, I knew," he accused, catching Dez by the wrist.

"Let me go!" Dez cried trying to pry her wrist loose from his painful grip. Realizing the futility of it, she began beating him with her free hand. It had no effect except to drive him insane at catching an open glance at her bare flesh.

"A pretty thing like you should learn to mind her manners," her stepfather teased through stained teeth. "And if your mother ain't up to teaching you a lesson, then I will." Catching her other wrist, he shoved her violently against the shower wall. Off balance Dez slipped on the wet surface, falling hard even as she grabbed for the shower curtain.

The first thought Dezzy had when she awoke was about the paint. She never recalled her mother repainting the bathroom. For as long as she could remember, the walls were nothing but a dull yellowish green. Years of smoking and steam muted the room's original colors. What they were Dezzy couldn't be certain.

Dezzy's second thought was about her location. She was no longer in the tub. Face up on the dirty, tiled floor, she was scrunched up against the base of the toilet. And wet.

Pushing aside her bangs, Dezzy rubbed her swollen eyes. The mist from the still running shower hung suspended. Unmoving. To her dismay, the entire bathroom was covered—no, splattered—in shades of red. She groggily sat up to find her stepfather dismembered at her feet — his entrails extending to the tub. He was torn open as if attacked by a wild animal.

Something within Dezzy stirred. But it wasn't until she looked at her hands that the shakes hit. Like her body, her hands were covered with a sticky crimson fluid.

Was it her stepfather's blood? Was it her own?

Dezzy attempted to rub the thick bits of flesh from her fingernails, but it was too much. The scene hit her stomach unannounced. She barely had time to lean over the tub as she emptied the contents of her stomach. What came up wasn't what she remembered eating.

After wiping herself down, Dezzy decided it was best to go to school. She'd deal with the surreal mess later. Quickly dressing, she made it to the bus stop just as the bus was rolling away.

By chance, the driver caught view of her in the side view mirror and momentarily waited for Dezzy to catch up. That's when Dezzy saw the deviant watching her in the side view mirror and stopped running. This wasn't the first time she nearly missed the bus. She suddenly became aware of how often it was happening.

The driver beeped the horn. He wanted her to run. Licking his lips in anticipation, he enjoyed watching Dezzy's breasts bounce out of control. Her nubile body excited him. But there was something different about Dezzy today. She met his stare in the mirror. Feeling ashamed, he averted his eyes, jumping in his seat when she pounded on the door to be let in.

"Took you long enough," he said as Dezzy climbed the stairs. His eyes darted from her face to her chest and then back to her eyes when he heard what sounded like a growl.

Her eyes narrowed as she smiled and grabbed for his face. In her right hand she held his mouth tight in her grip. Uncomfortably so. He tried to pucker his lips, thinking that's what she was doing. For a moment the driver thought she might actually kiss him. She instead applied more pressure until he winced in pain. "Hope you enjoyed the view because it's the very last time."

Letting go she stood up as the driver uttered a high-pitched cry and focused on not peeing himself after seeing something flicker in her eyes. Between that and the growling, he wondered if what he smoked the night before was tainted. Regardless, he went about finishing the route without a word or even looking in Dezzy's direction.

Once in her seat, the morning didn't improve. Watching Reggie, a boy she thought understood her, tongue some freshman chick on the ride in was almost more than she could handle. That he kept stealing glances over at her didn't help matters either. Both sophomores, they had been in the same classes together since middle school when she transferred in from another town. She had been crushing on him ever since. Interesting, she thought, how some twelve hours earlier Reggie sent her a text professing his undying love for her. Finally, after years of cat and mouse games, of guessing and waiting, he said what she was longing to hear.

Damn him for doing this to her, she thought as she played with her lip piercing, darting the tip of her tongue in and out of the loop. But then again, Reggie's text didn't stop Dezzy from meeting the guy from Tinder. Did Reggie know? Was this why he was torturing her so?

At school she couldn't get over how loud every noise seemed. She was hearing everything, including the whisperings of her English teacher, Mr. Susanu. He was talking about her to another male teacher, Mr. Dolion, someone she thought highly of until today.

"Look at her," Mr. Susanu was saying. "Little Miss Moody. Such a sullen little bitch. Damn kids have it all. What do they have to be depressed about?"

"I'm just curious about all her piercings," Mr. Dolion responded. "I mean, what's next?"

Susanu made a face. "Oh, please. She's probably already pierced her nipples and down there too."

Dezzy felt her face redden as she was forced to pass between the two men to enter her classroom. Their mocking smiles made her feel uncomfortable. Much like her stepfather delighted in doing daily. It boiled her blood. This wasn't how it was supposed to be with trusted male leaders. Especially trusted teachers who served as role models and counselors. They were supposed to make you feel safe. Protected from all that was bad in the world.

"Monsters. Animals. All of them," Dezzy muttered to herself. All of them except for Samael, that is. Samael, the 25-year-old from last night.

Entering her homeroom, she made her way to the back corner. Her usual spot.

"Hey, everyone! Look who decided to join us. It's Lezzy!" Brett chided.

"Kiss off!" she hissed.

Scrunched up in her seat, she nearly curled herself into a ball. Head down, her long hair easily helped to conceal what her black lace choker and red collared shirt already hid quite well—the hickey on her neck. Drawn up closely to her body, her long legs were accentuated by the black fishnet hosiery that extended from her black skirt of coffins and crosses. It was as if she was shielding herself from everyone in the room. In the world.

Homeroom ended quickly enough. As the students waited for first period to begin, they sat in cliques trading stories about the previous night's experiences online. Some talked about baseball and homework, some about the upcoming weekend, but mostly it was a class of whispers—the who's who of the latest rumors, hook-ups, and relationship wrecks.

Dezzy was deaf to it all, however, choosing to block it all out. She sat stewing, wanting to gut the boys in the room, beginning with Reggie. Stealing glances at the girls, fake in their flirtatious gestures, she decided she would tear them apart, too, limb from limb… posers all.

Suddenly Mr. Susanu was in her face. Screaming.

"Did you not hear what I said?" he repeated, his face an angry shade of purple.

Something was stirring deep inside Dezzy again. She chose to ignore it, instead wondering, as she observed the man in front of her, if it was possible for a human head to actually explode.

There was no acceptable way to respond. He was acting too irrationally. Dezzy merely blinked as she stared back at the man before her. Studying the lines on his face, she imagined burying her thumbs in his eyes to watch them ooze blood.

"Why, you little…" the teacher began, thrusting his finger threateningly in front of Dezzy's face. Her emotionless dead-eyed expression only exasperating him even more.

"Aw, c'mon Mr. Susanu. Say it," Brett encouraged grinning much too enthusiastically.

"It's easy to see why the youth of today will never amount to anything!" The teacher's voice reached a hysterical pitch as drops of spittle rained on the teenage girl.

Dezzy felt the stares of the class upon her. Keeping her head low, her eyes never left the teacher. And though she tried to fight whatever it was that stirred within her, she was no longer able to tame it.

The teacher turned his back to Dezzy for but a moment violently gesticulating to something on the chalkboard. Enraged, he continued his screaming and yelling. But Dezzy heard none of it. Just as he turned once again to confront her, she was airborne. As lithe as a cat, she was out of her chair. Her movements graceful. Effortless. Mr. Susanu barely had time to utter a feeble shriek before Dezzy pounced on his chest. In a blur of scarlet, his throat was torn wide open.

Gasping for air, the teenage girl's chest heaved. She winced at the rapid beating of her heart. Sluggishly her senses adjusted to the surroundings as she concentrated on catching her breath lest she pass out again.

Eyelids heavy, she could barely lift them. Even with great effort. Though her vision was somewhat blurred, the familiar muted yellow-green walls registered in her brain. Whatever dream or vision she experienced earlier already fading, she was once again on the dirty floor of her bathroom.

Naked.

Wet.

The water still sprayed from the showerhead behind her.

Through narrowed slits, the thick cloud of steam limited her sight. Yet she was able to observe her stepfather — once more alive — swallow back the remnants of his beer, crush the can, and toss it into the tub. Belching loudly, he wiped his mouth with the back of his hairy meaty hand before scratching his large, grotesque belly. Lecherous eyes ogled her frame as he smiled. If he had dared to look her in the eyes, he would have seen that she was conscious. Conscious and ready to fight back.

The swift kick to his groin caught him off guard. A former gymnast, her legs were still strong. Pools of water filled her stepfather's eyes as he reflexively clutched himself. His pained expression soon turned to one of rage.

"You slutty little bitch!" Cursing, the overweight man held himself with one hand while bending to reach for the girl with the other.

Balling up between the toilet and tub to avoid his touch, she delivered another kick. This time it connected with her stepfather's mandible. The force severed the man's tongue as his bottom jaw slammed against his upper row of teeth. An ejected bloody piece landed on her leg followed by thick raindrops of dark red.

The girl then kicked the man's right knee against the cacophony of his screeching. Given the weight it had to hold, it easily gave out from under him. Without time to react, down he went, striking his temple on the vanity countertop with a loud crack. It didn't take long before a shiny pool began expanding from under his head on the filthy floor.

Struggling to stand as the blood flowed towards her, the girl found she was already covered with it. Wiping it away, the blood seemed to splash everywhere as it ran like a river over her bare body the more frenzied she became. Navigating her stepfather's prostrate body to stand in front of the bathroom mirror, she waved away some of the mist before wiping the condensation from the glass.

Surprisingly, the blood covering her body wasn't her stepfather's. It was her own. The origin of the blood: the hickey on her neck. It bled in gulps. And as her breathing subsided, so did the seeping blood.

Examining the gory reflection of herself, spots of bright red were even on her lips. Lips that were now engorged unlike before. Running her tongue over the plump edges of her mouth, she tasted her own blood. An intense wave of ecstasy unexpectedly seized her, forcing her to grip the countertop in an effort to steady herself.

The teenage girl couldn't help but smirk at the discovery. She never felt more aware. More alive. More alert. Nor had she ever looked more radiant. Her smirk soon gave way to a wide, toothy grin revealing tiny fangs amid her upper and bottom rows of teeth. Admiring her new features, she was already beginning to overcome the melancholy she felt when she woke up. Absent was the feeling that something wasn't right or out of place.

Her stomach rumbled. Except for the pangs of hunger that grew with every breath, the earlier throbbing in her head was gone. It was time to get ready for school. After all, it was Friday. She was looking forward to seeing Reggie. Brett. The bus driver. Mr. Susanu.

But she'd have to satisfy her hunger first.

"Help me," the man on the floor begged with a faint whisper. "Please, Dez."

Good thing breakfast is ready, she thought to herself as she looked down at the blob that was her stepfather.

"My name," the girl said, dropping to straddle the man, "is Desdemona."

She placed her hands on her stepfather's wet skin and slid them up his spine while flattening herself against his thick back. Desdemona was able to pick up on subtle changes to his breathing and heart rate. Even in his injured state, he was still fully aware that there was a young naked girl on his back.

Desdemona inhaled his scent. Taking in the mixture of blood, sweat, and fear, she closed her eyes and moaned.

A searing warmth eased up her spinal column. She arched her back as she felt that warmth spread through her body. The tingling in her veins was almost too much. She shook her head to focus.

"But you, dear old dad," she added before feeding, "may call me Miss Paine."

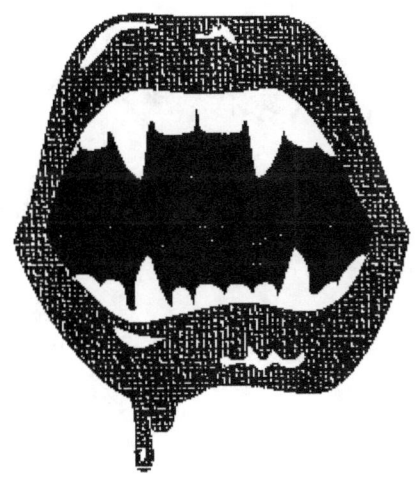

THE ORACLE BOARD

The planchette slid across the board with ease. Much faster than when any of the others were using it. That's why Aaron liked playing the board with Eli.

F. L. A. P.

"Flap? What does *that* mean?" Shelly asked. She peeked from behind her boyfriend, Aaron, who was sitting hunched over the board between her legs. His hands were on one side of the planchette.

Aaron shrugged. "Damned if I know. The spirits don't seem to want to talk much today."

Zeroed in on the board waiting to see if there was more to the message was Eli. His hands were on the other side of the triangular tool used to spell out messages from visiting spirits.

Shelly's roommate, Simone, tied her hair up in a ponytail. "Thought it always responded to you," she said looking at Eli. "That's what everyone's been saying."

It was a snowy Friday evening. A November Nor'Easter was bearing down on the area and the university where a dozen or so were holed up in Campo Hall, a first-year unisex dorm facility.

Simone slinked closer to Eli who was sitting pretzel-style across from Aaron. Atop of Aaron's roommate's bed, the board rested on the knees of the two playing the board.

Also on the top bed, sitting with his back against the wall, was Larry. Larry was crushing on Simone and enjoying the proximity. Though she was sitting to the left of Eli, she was up against Larry's leg. In between sips of Peppermint Schnapps, Larry couldn't get enough. Her pajama bottoms were riding low, exposing her underwear and a hint of the backend cleft.

Infatuated with her, Larry loved the way she looked. Loved how the mole on the back of her neck, only visible when she put her hair up in a ponytail, looked like the state of Maine. Loved the way she smelled. A mixture of some Avon brand perfume and cigarette smoke. Loved how she played hard to get. Perhaps it was the alcohol, but he was certain this was the weekend he had a shot with her. Why not? There was nothing else better to do to keep warm during a snowstorm. He even secretly hoped for a power outage.

Simone, however, barely registered Larry. There was someone else on her radar. Her breath warm on Eli's ear, she was about to say something before an inebriated Larry spoke up, his eyes closed and his head against the stone wall.

"Ask it what flap has to do with anything."

"Maybe it's referring to your girlfriend," Tim, Larry's roommate, said as he stood and grabbed for the schnapps bottle. He was the only one not on the bed.

Larry's eyes shot open as he turned three shades of red. So much for trying to impress Simone. "Ha ha. Very funny, butt breath."

Tim put the bottle aside for a moment so he could hold his right wrist with his left hand. He then rapidly moved his arm so his right-hand imitated flapping. "Flap. Flap. Flap."

"You guys really need to grow up," Shelly commented as she wrapped her arms around Aaron's chest and turned her head to rest her cheek against his back. She was getting sleepy.

"I got a great idea. Maybe we should use the board to call your ancestors. How about that, Tonto?"

Ignoring Larry's cheap shot aimed at his Native American Indian heritage, he took a swig from the bottle. "You're just jealous that my family automatically gets money from a casino." Eyes wide and grinning, Tim handed Larry back the bottle before his next zinger. "Hey, have you guys seen the *size* of the girl after Larry?"

Shelly spoke from behind Aaron. "Yes, you knuckle-dragging mouth breather. She lives up on the third floor near us. And if you weren't so focused on her weight, you'd see what a nice person she was."

Simone's lips were literally on Eli's neck. The smell of nicotine in her hair assaulted his nostrils. "Ask it again."

Tired of Larry and Tim, Aaron broke the concentration. "No, I think we're done for the day."

Tim threw his arms up in the air. "Aww, man. I was hoping to ask it some things."

"Yeah," Larry remarked, "How come we never get to use it?"

"We used it enough for the day."

"You guys have been using it all week. Like every day. All day," Larry complained before looking at Tim. "You and I have used it what? Maybe twice. What gives?"

Aaron looked at the two boys. "Yeah, and each time it's been the same thing. It doesn't work. Then you two bicker and complain."

"That's cause it's not real," Tim said, sounding jaded. "Besides, it's nothing like a spirit walk."

Eli stretched. "Oh, it's real all right."

"Says the faker it only works for. Wonder how you'd feel if I took you to a traditional Indian ceremony and everyone had visions but you."

Larry laughed, though it came out as a snort.

"Jesus, Tim. Like you've ever had visions yourself." Simone pushed Larry's legs aside so she could slide off the bunk. "It helps to know what you're talking about."

"I know exactly what I am talking about. My family is part of the Mashantucket Pequot Tribe."

"I'm sure they are. But don't act like you've *spirit walked* when you clearly haven't."

"Be thankful you guys weren't here the night before everyone went home," Shelly said. "They had three boards going at the same time in the room."

The thought of three boards going at once drew Larry's attention from Simone's backside. "No way! Really?"

"We still need to properly end the session," Aaron reminded Eli. "You always want to make sure to say good-bye. It's even better if they acknowledge. But no matter what, *you* need to."

Tim shook his head. "You guys are so full of crap. Okay, here's one for you. Eli, let's you and I do a session."

Aaron was the first to respond. "That's not a good idea."

Tim looked to Larry and made a face before replying. "Why not?"

"Because you'll piss off whoever we talk to," Eli answered.

Fed up, Tim waved them off. "I'm going to go watch some TV in the lounge." Then he looked to Larry. "You coming?"

Ignoring Tim, Aaron instructed Eli since this was the first time they ended a session together. Even though Eli took to the board easily throughout the week, he was using it when others were also playing. "Many people forget to do this. It is essential to close the door to the spirit world after a session. It should also keep any straggling spirits from hanging around. That's how hauntings begin. And, like a dog with a lot of energy that isn't given a chance to release that energy, spirits will become destructive if not told to leave. Make sense, Mr. Holy?"

Eli nodded before smirking. "Don't call me that."

"Pretty freaky watching you with this board. Never in my life have I seen anything like it. And to have the board call you 'too holy' gives me the creeps."

"I'm not sure about that. Didn't have much luck today."

"Well, were you focused or was your mind elsewhere? The mind needs to be clear when using the board. The spirits will take advantage of everything."

"I think I was distracted. My mom was upset that I didn't want to come home for Thanksgiving. Gave me a hard time about it too. But all my parents do is argue. So I came up with an excuse."

Simone chuckled. "You lied to your parents? I always took you for a goody two-shoes."

Aaron's tone turned serious. "Tim and Larry complain about the board but they don't take it seriously. And each time they've tried to use it they've been drinking. Whether you believe in it or not, it's dangerous and should be respected."

"I was also thinking about Tyler and Lazlo. So, wasn't really in the mood for family time."

"What about them?"

Shelly knew. "Lazlo's dog was attacked by something."

"Attacked? Oh, no. Is it okay?"

Shelly made a face and shook her head to indicate the negative. "The dog was found um... inside out."

Simone's stomach turned as she felt an unexpected sting of tears. "What? How come I didn't hear this? And how is that even possible?"

"No clue. But it was mutilated in some way. The story going around is the dog was hit by a car," Eli explained, "because they don't want to freak anyone out about it."

"And Tyler?" she asked.

"Hospitalized with alcohol poisoning. After using the board with us on Wednesday he went to an off-campus party. Family wanted to keep it quiet. Not sure how many who stayed behind know about it."

"Oh my God."

"I don't know if he's coming back on Monday. May not be for a while. I was going to call him on Sunday. Makes me wonder what forces we're dealing with. I didn't really ever look at the board as evil or good."

"Keep it that way," Aaron said looking at Eli, "and you won't invite the malevolent ones in. Besides, all of this could be a coincidence. Now, let's thank the spirits and say goodbye."

Simone wiped at her eyes and sighed. "It sucks that I missed everything this week. Can't believe what happened to Tyler and Lazlo. And you... I can't get over how you make that thing come to life."

"It was amazing *and* spooky. I've never seen the pointer move so fast as when Aaron and Eli use it. The other day it was Aaron and Eli on one. Lazlo and Tyler on another." Shelly turned to her boyfriend. "Aaron, who was on the third?"

"Guys from the residence hall next door. Not sure. Never met them before."

Shelly adjusted her socks after Aaron hopped off the bed. "Well, those pointers have never behaved that way when you and I use it. Someone even said they saw the boards glowing. Did you?"

"Not sure about that but I do recall the other two boards encountering some pretty hardcore entities. Suicides and a murder or something."

Everyone grew quiet until Eli swung his legs over the side of the bed. "What a week. What if the RAs get wind of us all playing with the boards?"

"They know already, I'm sure of it. So what if they do?" Aaron said making a face before leaning in to kiss Shelly. "They can't do anything about it."

"There's nothing illegal going on," Shelly added after Aaron removed his tongue from her mouth. "Not yet anyway."

"What is it?" Aaron asked noticing Eli's expression.

"Just weird, ya know."

"What is?" Simone asked.

"He's worried about Lazlo and Tyler. That there's a connection to what happened to them because they were using the board." Aaron then glanced over at Eli and smirked. "Am I right?"

"Well, they were using it a lot."

"You've been using it quite a bit." Aaron's expression changed. "C'mon now."

"Well, we're heading upstairs," Shelly announced. "So long as you don't tell Tim and Larry, you both are welcome to join us for some libations. Maybe we can also play a game or something."

Simone laughed and clicked her tongue. "Or something."

Shelly blew Aaron a kiss. "See you in a few."

"You, too, if you want," Simone seductively whispered in Eli's ear.

About an hour later when the door to his dorm room opened, Eli made no effort to conceal what he was doing. Why would he? Aaron apparently left the board for him when he was out of the room using the bathroom which Eli understood as Aaron wanting to use it again later. Maybe after the girls were asleep. In the wee hours of the morning. The witching hours.

But it was Eli's girlfriend, Bella, who walked in. Not Aaron. "Are you still playing with that thing?"

"Hey, you're back early," Eli said without looking up. "What thing?"

"The board, Einstein. I thought you were going to focus on your classes again."

"I am."

"So, what's this then?"

Eli looked up. "It's Friday night. Thanksgiving break."

"Yeah? And?"

"Bella, what's your problem? Why are you making such a big deal out of it? You're not even supposed to be here. You're supposed to be working. And then weren't you doing a sleep over with Tracey?"

"In case you didn't notice, there's a flippin' blizzard happening outside. They closed the store early and I decided I didn't want to spend the night with Tracey in Roby Hall. Thought you and I could spend the night together since your roomie went home for the turkey break. But I see you're too busy with that blasted board again. And if you weren't planning on me coming, then that means you were sneaking around behind my back."

"You make it sound like I've been using this for the entire semester. It's been a week, Bell."

"Yeah. We're lucky it's the Thanksgiving holiday. Enough's enough, though. Exams are right around the corner and this thing is an obsession. It's dangerous. Can't you see that?"

"It's fine." When his girlfriend rolled her eyes, he tried to convince her. "No, really. I'm *too holy*."

"It's not fine. And what does that even mean? Too holy?"

"Jesus, Isabella. What the hell do you want from me?"

"I want you to stop using it and go back to class."

"We're NOT in class! We got caught up using it earlier this week because there was nothing else to do around here and there's no one around. Most everyone left early. Those who are here are freakin' bored. Calm down."

"I thought you weren't supposed to use it alone."

"It's fine. Aaron left it in the room earlier. I'm just waiting for him. Anyway, I can't explain it to you because you're not there when we use it. But it's fine."

"Sounds exactly like what someone would say if they were getting possessed by it."

"Oh, my God. Really? You've seen way too many movies."

"I'm going upstairs to get my crucifix necklace that's been blessed by Father Millette and I am going to put it on this board while I say a prayer for you."

"Please don't."

"And I don't care if Shelly hates me after, but I'm also going to tell Aaron to keep this thing away from us."

"I wish you wouldn't. Why are you so insistent on starting trouble?"

"Look, if you're not going to dispose of it, then I don't want to be around you. You've changed since using it."

"I've changed? In a freakin' week?"

"Make up your mind what you want to do. Six months together and you never used language around me. Now it's eff this and eff that. You then sprinkle in some other colorful words. I'm sorry Eli, it's either me or the board."

"Bella, this is madness." Eli stood. "Tell you what. I'm going to take a walk. A breather. When I return, maybe you can stop being a bitch and we can—"

Bella didn't wait for Eli to finish his sentence. She instead picked up the board and broke it in two over the bed frame's footboard. "Sounds good to me."

"What the fuck did you just do?"

"See what I mean? You just proved my point."

"Seriously?"

"You're done. Or was I being too much of a bitch for you?"

"It wasn't even mine. It's Aaron's. He's going to… Jesus, I'm going to have to buy him a new one now."

Angry and frustrated, Bella stormed out of Eli's dorm room.

| 2 |

Eli pulled back the hoodie. He then removed the gauze covering Saturday night's freak accident in the dorm to examine the still-swollen area of his face. Thirty plus hours later, it painfully seeped throbbing gobs of red and yellow. Medical treatment for his facial wound and his hand weren't an option thanks to the Nor'Easter outside and its nearly fourteen inches of snow. The accident bore an unsightly gash to the cheekbone on the right side of his face. After nearly twenty Ibuprofen, there was no quelling the agonizing ache.

With slurping sounds, odd colored, foul-smelling seepage fell thickly into the sink as Eli massaged the pus engorged cheek. His attempt to drain it only resulted in a patch of extremely stretched translucent skin coming loose to hang in one heavily saturated bloody flap.

If only he heeded Aaron's warning.

"Yeah, whatever. Dude, I don't care..."

"Really, though, I'll get you another one. I promise."

"...about the board."

"Huh?"

"You don't understand. Listen to me. The board cannot be destroyed. And your girl is in grave danger."

"C'mon. Did you really just use the word *grave*? You don't believe that, do you?"

"Eli, did I ever tell you the history behind the board?"

"No."

"It's an old board. My great grandmother was the first to possess it. It's been in the family all these years because we cannot destroy it."

"You're serious?"

"Dead serious."

"So, you've never thrown it away?"

"Oh, no. You misunderstand me. My relatives have tried. Hear me? They've tried. They've driven to another state to dispose of it. They've buried it in a dump. They've thrown it in a chipper. Burned it. Didn't matter. Every single time it comes back."

The boys jumped when there came a knock at the door.

"Hey, whatcha guys doing?" Larry asked poking his head in the room.

"Not now," Eli said pushing against the door.

"Woo! It's Fornicatin' Friday, isn't it?" Tim yelled from behind Larry. "Is he in there with Bella?"

"Nah, just him and Aaron."

"Geez, you guys sure can't be separated from one another for too long, can you?"

Eli stepped aside as Aaron jerked open the door, causing Larry to spill into the room. "We have to find Bella."

"What? Why? What's going on?"

"You look pissed," Larry said when he saw Eli's face.

"I'm not pissed. Annoyed, maybe. But I'm not pissed. You heard Aaron. We need to find Bella. Wanna help?"

| 3 |

Eli was the first to wake up early Saturday morning. He was in Shelly and Simone's room on the third floor. Aaron was in the top bunk with Shelly snoring away. Tim and Larry were on the floor passed out using their coats as pillows. They still had their wet sneakers on. Eli realized he was in bed with Simone. Though clothed, it alarmed him.

"What are you doing?" Simone whispered as Eli reached for his sneakers.

"I'm going to go look again for Bella."

"She probably walked to Tracey's dorm."

"Middle of the night? In a blinding snowstorm with drifts of nearly two feet?"

"We girls do crazy things when we're angry."

"It doesn't make sense. She could have easily holed up here in her own room with the door locked if she was that angry."

"Uh huh."

"I just want to make sure she's okay."

"Sure you don't want to stay here where it's warm? We can all go looking with you when everyone gets up."

"I'm sure," he said grabbing his coat and quietly stepping out into the hall hoping he wouldn't get caught on the girls' floor during parietal hours.

Once in the hall he raced to the stairwell as he thrust his arms into the sleeves of his winter coat. Thoughts of last night's conversation with an angry Bella and then dreams he had of the board screaming out obscenities and threats as Bella tried to burn it only incited more fear in him.

Outside, it was difficult to get around. The wind wasn't helping at all. Once he cleared the drifts closest to the building and walkways with an overhang, everything else was buried under mounds of snow. Two feet in some areas, more in others. Because of drifts, in some places it was even higher. Much higher. With snow still coming down, it was going to be damn near impossible to find Bella.

But Eli didn't have to search far. After about eight or ten difficult steps in drifts that swallowed his legs, he tripped over something large and stiff between the walkway and the parking lot buried in the snow. Landing right on top of it, *it* was his girlfriend.

Stiff. Frozen. Dead.

But that's not even what scared him the most. It was her expression. Her mouth was wide open in a horrific silent scream. And her eyes were black hollow voids.

"Campus ministry. Please hold."

The phone lines were down all morning because of the storm. But now, early afternoon, it appeared the lines were back in working order. Spotty but working. Luckily for the students the school was on a main street. If only Eli had Tracey's number.

"Hello, Campus Ministry. How may I help you?"

"I was already on hold."

"Yes. Thank you for your patience. The lines have been pretty busy since they started working again."

"I was hoping to speak with a priest. Maybe Father Tony, if he's available."

"May I ask what this is in reference to?"

"My girlfriend just died."

"Bereavement. Okay. One moment."

Eli sat cross-legged on the floor with his back against his bed. He didn't know who else to call. He certainly didn't want to call his parents. He was also looking for some answers regarding how to deal with the board. Since the library was closed, he figured Father Tony might know. That is, if he took Eli seriously.

"Yes, hello. This is Father Tony. To whom am I speaking and what seems to be the problem?"

"Father Tony, it's Eli Manna. I live over in Campo Hall."

"Mr. Manna. Eli. Yes. You're often here on Sundays for our campus Spaghetti potluck. How are you, son? Faring okay in this white winter wonderland?"

"Actually, no. It's why I called."

"What's wrong, Eli?"

"My girlfriend, Father. She died."

"My goodness, Eli. I am so sorry. When did this happen?"

"Last night. Well, sometime early this morning actually."

"Wait, now. You wouldn't happen to be referring to the young lady they found early this morning outside Campo Hall, would you now?"

"Yes, Father."

"Oh, dear. I am so sorry. The university contacted me earlier this afternoon to be ready for calls from students. Said they'd like me to phone in on her parents, too. Because of the storm nothing is getting in or out of here. It's forecasted to last through Sunday now. Classes will most likely be canceled for the first couple of days of the week. Don't even know if paramedics will be able to retrieve her for a bit. Awful situation all around. How are you holding up?"

"Father, I think I know what killed her."

"Oh?"

"We had an argument."

"Over?"

"An oracle board. It's like a Ouija board."

"Okay."

"And I think it was the board that killed her."

There was a long pause before the priest spoke again. Eli thought for sure the line went dead and was about to hang up. "I must admit that's not what I expected to hear. What makes you certain that it was the board and not anything else? From what campus security shared, her death was the result of getting locked out of an empty dorm during a snowstorm. A random, though unfortunate, situation."

"The quarrel was over my using the board. And then she tried to destroy it."

"I see."

"Are you sure, Father? Are you even listening to me?"

Father Tony *was* listening. The priest was well aware, in fact, of the emotional roller coaster the boy was experiencing. "Son, are you aware that the planchette moves on account of something called an Ideomotor Response?"

"No."

"This response — phenomenon — is a psychological reflex in which a subject moves things unconsciously. In this case it would be the moving of the planchette. The concept is well known in the areas of hypnosis and psychological research."

"When I use it, it is *not* a reflex. It is definitely a response. It literally blows up when I use it. It races around the board like it has a mind of its own. It also provided the phrase that I was too holy. The movement of this thing is not based on any kind of reflex or motor response."

"Ideomotor Response."

"Whatever. It is a palpable response to our hands on the planchette. A response to our energy."

"I see. Well..." The line crackled before a person with Father Tony's voice returned. "Stupid. Stupid boy," the voice on the other end of the line charged. "You have no idea what you are dealing with."

"Father? Father Tony?"

"You've awakened something. Unleashed something dark. Evil. And it won't just be you who pays for it. Better pray for the little whore. Because of you, she's going to rot in hell. You, too, boy!"

Eli fumbled the receiver in his hands trying to hang up the phone. Cackling from the wicked voice could still be heard even after the line was disconnected.

Inconsolable, Eli couldn't stop shaking. That was not Father Tony. And he knew he was not dreaming. What he heard was real. It was a warning. A warning that only strengthened his resolve. He wanted to... he *had* to... make things right.

Aaron and the others tried checking in on Eli, but he kept his distance for the day. Especially after grabbing Simone by the throat in Bella's room. She just wouldn't lay off and kept coming on to him. That's when Shelly walked in. Her timing couldn't have been worse. Eli fled the room thankful it was Shelly and not Aaron who walked in on them. No doubt Aaron knew about the situation by now. Probably Tim and Larry as well.

But Eli couldn't think about that at this moment. He had a plan and no one was going to talk him out of it.

On the desk in his dorm room, Eli made his own talking board. Using pieces of paper with letters written on them, he set up a top arc. He then created another half-moon below with numbers. A shot glass would substitute for the planchette.

Eli recalled earlier in the week when there were about ten or twelve people crammed into Aaron's room, many of them taking turns working the three boards simultaneously. One of the guys from another residence hall knew someone who talked to their aunt after she died through a board.

"Word is the aunt answered questions no one sharing the planchette knew. It was a wild story. Scout's honor," the boy from the upperclassmen apartment building just up the hill said. "And this was right after she died. Like the next day."

Of course this story was contrasted with another from someone else about an eighth grade teacher who was an ex-nun. She claimed she once saw things floating in the air, levitating, and whipping about the room. Heavy stuff, too, such as furniture in addition to smaller things like ash trays and glasses. She strongly warned against using it.

And then there was the story of someone who fashioned their own board in very much the same way Eli just did. He was going to talk to Bella. Board or no board. He would talk to Bella tonight.

Turning off the lights, he lit a scented votive candle and moved it to the side of the desktop. But the shadows soon unnerved him. They came to life wildly jumping and dancing just beyond his periphery all while the flame of the candle burned rather unremarkably. That's how he knew they were alive. And every time he'd snap his head in the direction of the lively shadows they'd move far enough to be out of his line of sight.

"Keep it up. Keep trying to spook me. It won't work. Don't forget, I'm holy," he uttered aloud as a callback to a message a spirit spelled out on the board days earlier. Though he didn't feel at all holy, it seemed to explain why his effortless handling of the planchette gave it more life than anyone else who worked it.

Unsettled by the unnatural way the light and dark toyed with him, Eli got down to business flipping over the shot glass he planned to use as a pointer. Several times he attempted to place his fingers from both hands on the underside of the glass, but he was shaking so badly that he kept moving it.

Eli tried to shake off the dread that consumed him and took a deep breath before trying again. "Hello. I welcome the spirits who are in this room right now to communicate with me."

Nothing. Nothing but the rapid and loud thudding of his heart.

"I want to speak to Bella. Bella, I know you're here."

Still nothing. Eli licked his lips, tasting the salty sweat beading over his upper lip.

Hearing a commotion outside in the hall, Eli checked that his door was locked. He leaned his ear up against the door before hearing Larry and Tim's voices. No doubt they were drinking again. Probably with the group next door in the other residence hall. He held his breath as they passed by, hoping they wouldn't knock on the door.

Returning to the shot glass, he once more extended an invitation to the spirits in the room to communicate. There was only silence in return. No movement other than the flame of the candle and the shadows to remind him that something *was* there. It just wasn't cooperating.

After a pause long enough to find Eli giving in to exhaustion slumped over uncomfortably in his chair, the glass slowly nudged forward. Eli bolted upright in his seat certain he dreamed it. He must have since there were only two fingers of his right hand on the glass.

But across the desk the glass worked its way. When it neared the edge, Eli picked it up and placed it in the center of his improvised board. Whatever spirit was communicating with him wouldn't spell out any words. Instead it carved a path through the letters and numbers written on pieces of torn paper forcing Eli to stop and adjust everything several times over.

Looking at the time and feeling fatigued, Eli was quickly becoming impatient. And angry.

"I want to speak to Bella. Bella, you need to find your way to the board."

Maybe it wasn't going to any letters because the connection wasn't strong enough. Maybe it was because he was using a shot glass instead of a true planchette. Maybe it was because he was using it alone. Then the makeshift pointer stopped dead in its tracks.

"Dammit. Bella. I know you're here. It's too soon after..."

The glass inched forward again. Slowly at first. Then with some speed.

"Bella?"

Left to right. Then right to left. Again. Then again before making wide figure eights scattering the letters everywhere.

"You're here. Here and just as headstrong as when you were alive."

Eli broke the connection to once more adjust the paper letters on the desk. When he returned to the glass, it immediately moved to the letters *H... E... L...* "Yes, hello, Bell," Eli interrupted. "I should have listened to you. I know. You were right."

P... P... P... P...

"P?"

The pointer kept moving to the letter P before moving through all the letters.

"Dammit, Bell. I don't know what you're saying." Eli swept the paper numbers off the desk and arranged the letters from left to right so the visiting spirit could better spell out the messages. "How about we try this again?" he asked aloud hunched over the substitute pointer nearly out of breath.

Slowly the pointer crawled to the following letters: *I.N.H.E.L.U.K.I.L.D.M.E.*

"I don't under... No, this can't be right." Then as it spelled out the words again, Eli tried defending himself. "None of us knew what was going to happen."

H.A.T.E.Y.O.U.

The glass picked up speed repeating the same phrase: *H.A.T.E.Y.O.U.H.A.T.E.Y.O.U.*

"But you were the one who left. Why did you leave the dorm? There was a blizzard going on outside."

H.A.T.E.Y.O.U.H.A.T.E.Y.O.U. H.A.T.E.

"This is all *your* fault. You're the one who got on your high horse and broke Aaron's—"

Eli was cut off when the glass flew from his fingers and into the poster covered stone wall to his left. The force was so great that the glass shattered on impact.

Eli reflexively brought up his arms to shield himself. "I'm sorry. I'm so sorry," he cried putting his head into his hands terrified.

When the flame of the tiny votive candle brightened, Eli didn't think much if it at first. Not until his brain registered what it had been witnessing throughout the week and especially in the last hour. He reached out for the candle to extinguish it when it vibrated and fell onto its side. Spattering hot wax everywhere, it just missed his hands. Yet the wick still burned.

"I don't know what you want me to do. What do you want from me, Bella?"

Almost as if in response the tiny scraps of paper burst into flames and were airborne the more Eli waved his arms about and reached for the candle holder to upright it. That's when he heard it crack. The glass holder splintered into a thousand shards before exploding in Eli's face.

| 4 |

The exposed raw flesh stung as if pricked by a thousand tiny needles at the same time. Horrified by the loose skin hanging from his cheek, Eli decided to give it a pull. But instead of coming free, he pulled a newly raw line down to his jaw.

Blood soaked his hands. Leaking from the exposed flesh, it dripped over his chin and pooled all over the bathroom counter.

Frantic now, Eli pulled again. This time he ripped a raw strip under his bottom lip across his chin to the other side of his face. Blood drops dotted the mirror. The flap of loose skin, the consistency of melted mozzarella cheese atop a pizza, hung down to his chest.

Staring back at himself, it was difficult to recognize the person — no, the thing — in the mirror.

Angry. Frustrated. In unimaginable pain, Eli grasped the slippery handful of flesh with both hands and yanked outward hard and fast. The pain almost forced him to his knees. He succeeded in finally pulling the flap free. But to his horror he also succeeded in removing most of the skin from his face.

In the mirror's reflection was someone he *once knew* as Eli. In its place, a ghastly doppelganger. One whose face was now skinless. Not

even human looking. He didn't think it was possible to remove so much skin. Even acci-
dentally.

He smirked at the absurdity of the situation.
Exposed were his facial muscles and nerves.
Eyeballs suspended by tendons in moist sockets. Eli regarded the heavy flap of skin in his
hands with curiosity. That's when he noticed the
board on the counter to his right. Aaron's board.
Intact. Whole. Solid. Even though Bella had broken it into two pieces. The wooden planchette
was there too, pointing to the eye on the board.

When his own eyes found his reflection once
more in the mirror, a demon — a devilish imp
with giant wings — stood near his left shoulder.
Then a familiar face appeared behind his right
shoulder. On her face was the same gruesome
expression as when he found her in the snow.
Cold purple arms wrapped around his chest as
she tilted her head and stared at him with a
ghastly open-mouthed expression and liquid
black vacant eyes.

MABEL

Darnell was playing basketball on the outskirts of the city not far from an abandoned apartment complex. It was a ratty court but he liked the sound the chain nets made. Long forgotten, the area was vacant and littered with trash. Graffiti covered the buildings on the nearby property. There was even graffiti on the cemented surface of the court.

Darnell enjoyed having the court to himself. It was here he came to think and get away from things at home. And at school. Being away from the noise also helped soothe the chronic headaches he suffered lately.

Though a part of Darnell wished he could do more to protect his mother from her new suitor, he already carried enough guilt for not doing enough to help her and his younger sister when they were all with his dad.

To avoid the ongoing drama at home now between his mom and her abusive boyfriend, Darnell made sure to stay as far away as he could. This morning it was especially bad. He decided to head out early. Only he wasn't going to school. He was certain his teachers would read his body language and start asking all sorts of questions. So he skipped. It wasn't like it mattered much anyway since wherever he was he felt overlooked.

It was a crisp fall day. Not yet cold enough for snow but perfect for a hoodie and jeans. Hands didn't get too cold. Ball gripped well. He'd hang at the court until around lunch. Then he'd hit Busters, where Gentleman George, as they called him, would hook him up with something to eat. For the rest of the day he planned to walk the tracks and then hit the local library once school was out so no one would sic a truant officer on him.

On a roll, Darnell moved back a step farther with each shot from the foul line until he was at half court. Every ball made it through the eye of the basket. Except for the last one.

The ball bounced free of the enclosure through a hole in the fence. Darnell took off after it. The ball seemed to bounce forever and ended up in a creek not far from a dozen other balls. By the smell of it, the creek was more like a storm drain runoff. To get to his ball, Darnell had to maneuver saturated mud and discarded litter. The last thing he wanted to do was to get the stuff on his sneakers. He loved his kicks. It was one of the first things he bought with money he saved up.

Darnell held his breath. The area was clearly a dumping ground and not just a collection of things caught up in the drains. Marlboro cigarette boxes. Swisher Sweet wrappers. McDonald's bags. Dirty diapers. Toys and stuffed animals. A couple of Barbie dolls. Clothes, too. Dresses and a lot of undergarments.

Debris was scattered up and down the gulley. Kicking over a pair of abandoned sneakers resembling a pair he wore, Darnell noticed a crumpled piece of paper roll out into the muck. He unraveled the balled-up paper, smoothing it out over his knee.

"Gross!" he uttered as he wiped the sludge from his hands onto the leg of his jeans.

On the paper was a hastily written letter composed in ink.

my name is mabel and momma and i are trapped in apartment 303 at Hartford village commons, we can't leave and we are in danger. if you find this please help us.

Darnell vaguely remembered reading about something happening at Hartford Village Commons, the apartment complex near the basketball court where he shot hoops. He knew it to be abandoned some years back, though he wasn't sure why. A large complex of multiple buildings was planned but only two were ever completed. Touted once as one of the nicest, safest places to live, it quickly fell into disrepair. Maybe it was because the focus of the city moved to the east side due to the poor economy.

Darnell wondered what Mabel looked like. If she was still there. He wondered how long ago she wrote the message that ended up in the sneaker. And if the message was even real. In all the times he hung out at the courts he never came across anyone. Certainly not any children.

Because the letter could be a clue to a missing person's case or an unsolved murder, Darnell considered alerting the police. He didn't want to get in trouble, so he decided to assess the situation firsthand. Then he'd inform the police. Maybe.

Since it was still early yet, Darnell made his way over to Hartford Village. He pumped his bike as fast as it could go under the fast-moving gray clouds that threatened rain.

Made up of two low-rise decrepit structures, Hartford Village Commons was surrounded by overgrowth reclaiming what were once manicured lawns, a flower garden, and an area for kids to play. The trees on the property, rotted and naked of any leaves, were twisted and black. A smaller front building, just over the walkway, appeared to be a maintenance building judging by the tools and traps visible through the broken windows.

Taking in the shape and condition of the larger buildings, Darnell noticed something shining in one of the upstairs windows. A reflection? A trick of light? It certainly wasn't the sun. It was mid-morning and yet the overcast skies made it feel late afternoon.

Since abandoned buildings were often a haven for drifters, there was a chance what he saw was a room occupied by a squatter. Scratch that. Squatters. Plural. He looked around at the state of the grounds. Trash everywhere. Junked cars. Mattresses. Overturned dumpsters. Determining it wasn't safe, he thrust his hands into his pockets and turned around to go home.

But then he felt Mabel's note under his fingertips. Darnell ran up to the entranceway and pushed open the doors letting curiosity get the better of him. Inside the building was dark. Musty. The little bit of daylight serving as the only source of illumination managing to sneak through broken windows.

He tried random light switches already knowing the result. As his eyes adjusted to the dim lighting, he took in the area. The lobby was still furnished but everything was covered in filth and grime. Papers, folders, and trash were everywhere amid the dirt and leaves. Darnell got the impression the building was abandoned at a moment's notice. He wondered if something bad happened. Perhaps to the building. Maybe the area. The residents.

Just as Darnell was determining what to do next, movement caught his eye. He advanced deeper into the lobby, past the mailboxes on the side wall, hoping to catch a glimpse of whatever was in the building with him.

Extracting a Zippo lighter from his pocket, he ignited the flame while heading for the stairwell. Mabel's apartment was supposed to be on the third floor.

The stairs in the stairwell were decaying and the banisters looked unstable. Graffiti marked the peeling walls. Heedlessly deciding it was safe enough, Darnell put out of his mind what could happen if the staircase collapsed.

As he climbed, strange noises echoed in the stairwell. Were there people occupying the floors? It wasn't difficult to get in. It suddenly occurred to him that the front door wasn't even locked. Though some windows were boarded up, the front door was very easy to navigate. That meant there was no telling what danger lurked inside the building. He could get shanked and no one would know he was here. It was one of the reasons why he never liked going into the crowded part of the city. He feared getting jumped. Mugged. Or stabbed. Even the city bus was rough depending on the time of day it was ridden.

Reaching the third floor, it was eerily quiet. Illuminating the hallway was light from windows at both ends of the hall. But the air was clouded in dust. The slow floaters resembled spores from a horror film.

Darnell began checking the apartment numbers on the wall for 303. When he found the place, the door to it was slightly ajar. "Hello? Anyone home?" He was about to knock when he heard movement. "Hello?"

As he grabbed for the handle, the door opened wider. An older man in a windbreaker and baseball cap rushed the boy. "You shouldn't be here."

Darnell stepped aside unsure of the approaching man's actions. He then called after him. "Where's Mabel?"

"Don't know who that is and don't care."

Darnell noticed the man's dirty brown loafers and something white in his hands. "Is this where Mabel lives? She here?"

"Go away. You're not wanted. There's nothing for you here."

Darnell poked his head inside the apartment. Even overcast, enough light from the windows revealed a tidy place covered in shag brown carpeting. Hung on walls of mostly paneled wood were paintings of African art. There was a painting of a black Jesus. Zulu masks adorned either side of the hallway entrance to the bedrooms where Darnell recognized framed photos of Dr. Martin Luther King and Malcolm X next to what looked like a collage of family photos.

A little girl in a pretty but torn white dress emerged from behind the sofa. She appeared bruised.

"Are you okay?" Darnell asked running over to her.

"You really shouldn't be here," she said walking by him dismissively and into the kitchen. She opened the fridge to remove a container with colored liquid. Pulling a stool over to the counter, she hopped up and acquired a glass from the high cupboard. Once down, she poured herself a glass of the red water holding the container with two hands.

"What are you doing? Is that even cold?"

Only after she took several gulps did she answer. "Having Kool Aid," she said looking at Darnell with red stained lips.

"Are you Mabel?"

"You already know who I am."

"My name is Darnell. My family and friends call me DJ but by dad used to call me Junior."

"Momma and I are in danger here. Can you help me leave?"

Darnell glanced from her to the open door. "Not sure that's going to be much of a problem. Seems you can easily walk out of here if you want to." Looking more closely at the girl's torn dress and bruises, it wasn't too hard to connect the dots. He thought of his deceased sister. Was reminded of what his own dad did to her. "Yeah. I'll do whatever I can. If you want me to walk out with you, I will. If that's what you want."

"I want to leave," she repeated. She placed her glass down and wiped her mouth with the back of her hand. Even against her dark skin, the red stained moustache was visible. And there to stay. Replacing the cap to the container, she returned it to the refrigerator and then stood staring at Darnell.

"Oh, okay. Let's go. Lead the way."

But the girl didn't budge. "Is he out there?"

Darnell made a face. "Who?"

"The keeper," she replied.

"Who?"

"The keeper. Is the keeper still out there?"

"You mean the guy with the ball cap that was just here?"

"Yes. The keeper. He was trying to hurt me."

Darnell was beginning to get the picture, even if some of what was happening didn't make sense. Was this Mabel? What did this man, this keeper guy, want with her?

Darnell gestured for her to wait until he checked the far end of the hallway and its stairwell. Then he checked the one closest to her apartment.

"Okay," Darnell began, about ready to inform the girl that the coast was clear before she sprinted through the open door. As she pranced eagerly down the hall, Darnell chased after her, barely keeping up until she stopped in front of the door leading to the stairwell.

Fingers intertwined in front of her, she hummed rolling from her toes to her heels waiting for Darnell to catch up. But once Darnell caught up with her, she sprinted past him heading back towards the apartment.

"Where are you going now?"

"I forgot something."

When she returned, Darnell noticed she was holding on to a worn stuffed animal of some kind. He squatted in front of her before she could advance down the stairs. "If anything should happen again, run as far and as fast away from here as you can. There's a police station a few blocks not far from the highway."

"Momma says we can't trust the police. And that they won't believe me."

The girl wasn't wrong, but Darnell didn't know what other options were available. He still believed it to be her safest choice should they become separated. "I know the feeling, but I think you should still try. Look for a dark officer."

She just stared at him blankly, blinking her big brown eyes.

"And I'm sure you already know this but there is a cream-colored building just beyond the swing in the front."

"That's where the keeper goes."

"It is? Well, besides avoiding that creepy man, I'd also stay clear of the building. There are a lot of sharp tools in there." Darnell stood thinking of his deceased sister. "Seriously, Mabel."

"Yes?"

"If that man ever comes near you again or tries to hurt you, you make sure to fight back. You scream. Yell. Kick if you have to. Grab a rock, a key, scissors, a knife... And you fight back. As hard as you can. Got it?"

"Okay," she said. Then Mabel was off, laughing with childish glee as she bounded down the unsafe stairs, her dirty disfigured doll bobbing violently in the hand holding it. Darnell trailed after her. But she was already a level below, a blur leaving giggling echoes in her wake.

With each set of stairs, she seemed to move farther ahead of him. Once out into the lobby, Darnell caught a glimpse of her exiting the main doors. He ran after her to catch up. Yet outside there was no Mabel to be seen. She seemed so fearful of the groundskeeper there was a part of Darnell that wanted to protect her until...

Until what? he thought to himself. Under the gray clouds he questioned what would even be next. He was certain the pay phones on the corner didn't work, like everything else around here. One of them was even missing its cord. Would she walk with him to the east end where they'd be able to find a police station? Would he be blamed for her bruises?

The dirty grounds surrounding the buildings were just as deserted as when he arrived. She could be anywhere. He called out her name, but there was still no sign of Mabel. It was as if she vanished into thin air.

As Darnell stood looking around in confusion, an older black man wearing a custodial uniform appeared chomping on a small cigar. His slacks and coat were a darker gray than his collared shirt. "Still looking for Mabel, are ya?"

Still? Darnell shuffled in place uncomfortably. "I'm sorry. Who are you?"

"I'm the groundskeeper."

Darnell noticed the man looked a lot like the one who brushed past the boy earlier. He looked down at the shoes. They were the same muddied loafers he saw on the figure leaving Mabel's apartment upstairs. Darnell's eyes were wide as he shifted his gaze from the man's shoes to his face.

"Girl just disappeared, am I right?"

"How did you know?"

"It's always the same." The keeper removed a nearly expired cigar from his lips and tapped the ash end before returning it. "A certain someone finds a message and it directs them to come here. They meet Mabel in her flat. Feel sorry for her. Help her leave. Before long Mabel is back in her apartment, once again waiting to be rescued."

"Why does she end up back there?" Darnell asked while also wondering why two abandoned buildings needed a groundskeeper.

"Because that's where the poor girl lives. It's where her momma told her to stay until she come back."

"But she hasn't come back, has she?" Darnell studied the older man in front of him. He looked to be in his fifties. Receding gray kinked curls covered his head. A thick gray-haired caterpillar covered his upper lip. He was paunchy but had the strong sturdy hands of someone who worked physically for a living. "And she's *not* coming back, is she?" Darnell deduced feeling a chill.

The man before him smiled slyly as he maneuvered the cigar stub from one side of his mouth to the other. He appeared to be chewing on it. "For a ghost, you're pretty slow to catch on. Figured you'd already known since you and I done have this conversation before."

"I've asked you about Mabel before?"

"Punk ass been comin' around a lot lately."

Darnell ignored the man's foolish talk. "What's Mabel to you?"

"Seems she's been recently awakened. Opened herself up to all kinds of supernatural. Like you, for example?"

"I — I don't understand. How?"

Again the keeper smiled. Smiled coyly as he puffed away on the last draws of his stogie.

"Oh, my God. What have you done to her?"

"It's not what I've done, boy. It's what I'ma gonna do," the man said as he withdrew the wet nub from his mouth and tossed it aside.

Darnell charged the keeper only to pass right through him.

"What up there, fine thang?" he heard the groundskeeper say to an attractive younger woman accompanied by two other young girls in their teens. He subtly placed a bag of something in her hand as she walked by.

Suddenly the promenade came to life. The area bustled with city folk wearing bell bottoms and tight jeans. There was brown leather. Afros and long sideburns. Hoop earrings. Faux fur and leopard prints. Toothy grins. Joyous banter set against music coming from the apartments and the decked-out speakers in the cars parked in the lot.

Green grass and wide-open spaces replaced the dreary compound strewn with rubbish Darnell was used to seeing. Kids laughed and played on the swing set and climbed the healthy trees full and lush with leaves. Even the skies transformed, changing from gray and foreboding to a striking blue. Not one cloud could be found in the sky.

Darnell closed his eyes and inhaled deeply. He smelled home cooking. There was no mistaking it. So many delectable smells coming from all directions. For someone who fancied being alone, seeing all sorts of black and brown folk living life to the fullest made him wish he could be part of the vibrant culture he was suddenly witnessing. Unlike the creepy groundskeeper, unlike his mother's new boyfriend or what he remembered of his dad, these were good people. He could tell just by the way they interacted with each other. The way they carried themselves. They were happy. Thriving.

"What just happened?" Darnell asked as he shadowed the groundskeeper across the front lawn to the small building by the street.

"The same thing that always happens, boy." The keeper pulled on the ring of keys attached to his belt. He was about to unlock the door when he remembered it was already unlocked.

And ajar. "You finally realized you's dead. Instead of just latching on to Mabel, you now seein' the entire block."

"I don't understand. Why is it then that *you* can see me?"

"You're obviously here for a reason. Mabel is maybe the main reason. Reckon there may be another. So, let me help you out there, kid." Before stepping into the maintenance building, the man pulled back his coat to reveal his name tag.

"That can't be. There's gotta be a mistake." Darnell shuddered as a shiver ran the length of his spine. If his head didn't suddenly hurt so badly, he wasn't sure if he'd scream or cry.

The keeper spit out remnants of the tobacco still on his tongue from his cheap cigar. "I done already told you to leave, Junior."

Terror suddenly consumed Darnell as the words from the man in front of him confirmed the name that was on the tag. Only his dad ever called him Junior. "No. You don't get to call me that."

"Told you to leave when's you were alive. That you weren't wanted. You didn't listen. Done got yourself hurt gettin' there all up in your old man's business." The man extracted the last cigarette stick from a small red and white box he pulled from his shirt pocket. As he spoke, the agitation was noticeable in his voice and in his crushing of the box before tossing it aside. "Here you are now a spirit of some sort and still just as pigheaded and dumb as you were alive.

Now git. Get to dyin' and passin' on or whatever it is you needs to do."

It occurred to Darnell that the evil man before him wasn't just standing in front of the door to the maintenance building. He was blocking it. "Mabel's in there, isn't she?"

"You like a little black Casper, you know that. Maybe I'll gets myself a priest 'n exorcise your sorry ass since I can't crack the other side of that skull of yours."

The keeper reached into his coat pocket and removed a 1940s era Zippo lighter. With an upswing of his thumb, he flipped the top open. He then ignited the large flame to light his cigarette on the downswing just as he turned to step into the building. But Darnell's dad didn't see the young child holding an open rusted gasoline can she found on the shelf or the nails scattered over the floor.

Mabel shook the can at the man, dousing him with the flammable liquid before throwing it at him. It only took a moment for the groundskeeper to become a walking inferno.

Darnell watched the horrific scene unfold with widening eyes wishing there was more he could do. "Mabel! Get out of there!"

Screaming, Darnell's father no longer sounded human. Inside the small building he inched closer to Mabel stepping on the nails and swinging his arms blindly. "I'll get you for this," he threatened knocking over tools and tripping over things on the floor. But she cowered in an area beneath a workbench until she saw her moment.

Mabel leapt up and emptied what remained of the other gas cans. "Like my momma says, you is evil. You're not going to bother us ever again."

The lumbering groundskeeper, blind and in pain, dropped hard to the floor, the nails piercing his flesh as the flames consumed him.

Mabel ran out and away from the building. A series of small explosions blew out the windows and destroyed the inside, including part of the roof. It crumbled onto what was left of the once human groundskeeper.

Mabel and Darnell watched the building burn before she turned to him. She was the only person who could see or hear him. "I did like you told me. I fought back. You won't have to visit me anymore. I will be okay. You can be free now."

People heard the explosions. The site of a bruised nine-year-old wearing a tattered white dress covered in soot was also drawing attention. People dropped what they were doing and rushed in on the young girl. A man was on the pay phone calling the police.

"I seen you before, you know. Before you died. Before you started visiting me. When you and your sister lived with your daddy here in the building. You were always nice to me and Momma. Momma was always grateful for the time you found me by the sewer."

The girl was crying now, though she tried not to. "Momma sad for so long when you didn't come home. Knew what happened but couldn't say anything. Knew what happened to your sister too. She was scared. We was also in danger. But you saved me, DJ. Again."

Darnell's form was beginning to glisten. There were so many things he wanted to say to the little girl. So many questions that initially seemed important. But that was before he felt himself being pulled. Pulled to another place. And then he was gone.

With tears in her eyes, Mabel waved goodbye as the community of Hartford Village Commons gathered around her.

HEAR MORE

The younger priest put one hand on the other's back and one hand on his arm to steady the older man. "What is it, David?"

"I don't kn—. It's… it's nothing," the elder priest said to his colleague. "Just suddenly woozy is all."

"You feel something, don't you?"

Father Tomassi stopped walking and took a deep breath. "I don't know, Joseph. Not sure if it's a feeling or if I am sensing something. I'm hoping it's an old age moment."

Joseph looked around for a place where they could sit. Spotting a bench near a life-sized statue of Mary, the Virgin Mother of Jesus Christ, he urged they take a moment to gather themselves. "How about we say a prayer before we go in?"

Tomassi patted Joseph's hand and smiled, grateful to be accompanied by the young man. "Good idea."

Your mother weeps for you, Alejandro. Cries out for you. She wants to know why you abandoned her when she needed you most.

Father Alejandro shook off the serpent's voice in his head as he clawed at his ears.

How could you do that to the very person who carried you in her womb for ten months? Does life mean so little to you that you would abandon the person who brought you into this world during a time of her suffering?

"Alejandro, my son, why have your forsaken me?" His mother sobbed. "Where are you? It's so cold here. So dark."

We can't wait for you to join us, the demon announced as Alejandro heard his mother scream out in agony for him.

The loud thud upstairs in the rectory drew Father Tomassi's attention. He turned his focus from setting the dining room table to getting up the stairs as fast as he could.

Once on the second floor, he knocked on the closed door. "Father Alex, are you okay?" When there was no answer, he announced his intention and entered the visiting priest's room.

"I'm good. It's nothing," Father Alejandro said when Tomassi found him on the bathroom floor. "It will pass." He was white. Shaking. And drenched in sweat.

"Dear Jesus, what happened?"

"Just slipped... Please. Give me a few minutes and I will be down for dinner. I'm good. It's okay."

"I'm so sorry for your loss, David." Joseph and Father David Tomassi stood in the small nondescript room that was once Father Alejandro's. "Will you be attending the service in Rome?"

"I'm not certain there will be one."

"Why is that? He worked directly for the Vatican, did he not?"

Father David Tomassi exited the room to check the hallway before returning to lean into Joseph. "Unofficially."

"Oh, I just thought..."

"I'm not even certain Pope Pontius is truly sanctioning these efforts."

"You think something else is in the works?"

"I think it's a way for him to keep track of the growing evil threat but under the radar."

"You think he knows about the Easter Massacre at the hospital?"

"How could he not? The question is *how much* he knows. Regardless, I don't know that we should take any chances."

"There aren't any other organizations working secretly within the Church that he may not be aware of, are there?"

"I don't know, Joseph. I'm not even sure Bishop Reibold knew either."

Father Tomassi was giving the room a final look over. There were three boxes on the bed belonging to the deceased: a box of clothes, a box of books, and a box of personal effects.

Joseph thought it odd that only the personal effects box was sealed. "This is everything?"

"Yes."

"He left this all to you?"

"He did," Tomassi answered as he folded the four flaps of the cardboard box containing Father Alejandro's clothes.

"Let me help you," Joseph said holding the flaps down while his friend taped the box shut with the last of the tape.

"Thank you. I only knew Father Alex for a short time. Met him not long after we lost Simon." Alerted to movement in the hall, Father Tomassi looked at his watch. "I think Sister Leslie is back. Would you excuse me? I shouldn't be much more than ten minutes or so."

"Of course. I'll put the boxes in the car while you're in your meeting."

"That would be great. Thank you."

Joseph was admiring Alejandro's book collection when he suddenly felt Tomassi's hand clutching his wrist.

"Jesus, Mary, and Joseph! What have you done!"

Joseph shrieked. "What? What did I do?" Trembling, he was feeling incredibly embarrassed. And alarmed by his friend's uncharacteristic behavior. "David, I was just looking at Alex's books. I swear. I thought you were going to meet with Sister Leslie."

"That's just it. I did." Tomassi's expression panicked Joseph. "It's been nearly half an hour."

Feeling awkward and unsure of what was happening, Joseph shook his head.

"You don't remember, do you?"

"I told you I was just looking at Father Alex's books when you walked out of the room."

Tomassi let go and eased his friend away from the bed. "Look down."

Joseph did just that only to find that he wasn't in the book box. He was in the effects box. Unsealed, the tape was ripped apart and the lid removed. "Dear God, David. I'm so sorry. I… I don't know what happened."

"Father Alex was an exorcist. That's what happened. It is exactly why certain things need to be handled very carefully. It is why the box was sealed, not just taped. I'm the one who is sorry. I should have never left you in here with the box. See that there special seal? Someone knew enough to seal it before a special Vatican envoy comes to collect it."

"That's what your meeting was about, wasn't it?"

"Yes. Remember how we felt coming in. Sister Leslie's been feeling the same. She wants the boxes out of here and would prefer we deal with the envoy." Tomassi turned Joseph's hands over. "You didn't touch anything, did you?"

"I don't know. I don't think so."

"It's how spirits find their way into our world."

"Through someone's personal effects?"

"Items belonging to an exorcist have to be handled very carefully. There's always a chance the items may have had contact with demonic spirits."

Joseph was beside himself feeling weak. "Why the draw, David? I mean, I used to be a priest. I pray regularly. I'm right there with Sarah taking care of her son, Jason Christopher. There's no temptation. What did I do?"

"It may not have been you. I may have been the conduit through my association with Alex. Maybe that activated something or woke something up. I'm not sure. And it may have something to do with what's in the display case. You're sure you don't remember touching anything?"

"For what it's worth I don't. But I don't know. What's in the display case?"

"Would you believe hearing aids?"

Joseph leaned forward to look into the box as Tomassi promptly replaced the lid. Whatever was in the case had to be small. Too small to be hearing aids. "Never seen devices that look like that. New tech? Foreign?"

"Neither."

"Then what?"

"Possibly supernatural."

It was a dark overcast day. Brisk. Not unlike the day he met Simon Free. His nephew's father. The man who sacrificed himself during the Easter Massacre of 1980 to give the world more time before End Times.

"I thought I was the only one lost in my thoughts."

The elder priest chuckled. "First, thank you, Alex, for joining me this morning. The Holy Spirit was strong with the two of us presiding over the 10 AM mass."

"My pleasure, David. And it was an honor to shake hands with your congregation."

"They mean a lot to me. Not many people come to mass anymore, as you saw."

"Indeed. We are experiencing darker times."

"A definite dark awakening to be certain."

"That's kind of why I am here. Fancy a walk around the grounds rather than sitting inside?"

Father Tomassi inhaled deeply and descended a few steps as he buttoned up his coat. He looked forward to their discussion since dinner the night before was awkward and mostly silent. "Splendid idea."

Across the street situated between the rectory on the right and the convent on the left was a Catholic elementary school.

"How are your numbers?" Father Alejandro

asked as they crossed the street.

"Steady. For the younger grades. By the time they're ready for middle school, many are opting for the public school up the road."

"Ahh."

"Well, new building, too."

"Latest technology, no doubt."

"More resources, too."

"Yes, indeed. Let's not forget cheaper as well. Always the elephant in the room when it comes to keeping our buildings open and our parishes operational. People are, after all, already paying taxes. Thus, the community begins to overlook the value of a parochial education because of the extra expense."

Rounding the back of the building there was a bench that the elder priest motioned to. "How about here?" He continued after they sat. "Times are still tough for a lot of people. And it doesn't help when our congregants bear witness to false prophets."

"Meaning?"

"I'm just a firm believer that we should live as we preach. I'm saddened to find many of our brothers are not. And at the expense of their sisters and the parish as a whole."

The visiting priest padded Tomassi's arm. "All humans are fallible. Still children of God, though."

"Which is why, Alex, it is imperative that we *live* the Word as much as spread it. I see the attitudes and faith slipping more and more. So many are clueless."

"I suppose you are correct. The struggle is real. For all. I see it every day. You came into the profession later in life, did you not?"

"I did."

"I'm curious. As a person of the Church, ever hear voices?"

"Depends on what you're referring to. Do I hear voices I don't want to? Or are you asking if I hear God speaking to me?"

Father Alejandro looked over at Father Tomassi and nodded before he smiled. "Both."

The white-haired priest grimaced. "I feel there are times I hear God... but He usually speaks through others. Or through situations. Regarding the more unpleasant voices, they tend to come in dreams. Not sure if that helps."

"It does. I'm just... I don't know. It's going to sound strange."

"You're here. Might as well come clean about what it is you are experiencing. It's the only way I can truly be of any assistance."

"I always knew I wanted to be a priest, you know. Felt the calling to serve as young as second or third grade. My formative years were spent in a school not much different than this one."

"But?"

"Well, I don't know. I thought the calling was to become a teacher via the collar. Volunteer at missionaries. Teach young and old. That kind of thing. So after seminary I went into teaching."

Tomassi's eyes lit up. "Wonderful. A noble profession. Too bad we couldn't get you to come to our school. What grade?"

"Seventh."

"A transitionary year. No longer a child, not yet a teenager. Tough age."

"But a good age. A good age."

"How long have you been teaching?"

"I taught for only a few years. I mean, I guess we're always teachers, right? But my life changed following a very traumatic experience with a possessed student."

"Oh, my. I'm sorry."

"Spent nearly a decade after praying on it. Processing. Studying. Observing."

"Was it a sanctioned exorcism?"

"No. Received blowback from some very important members of the diocese in fact. Blowback that was the ripple effect of a tongue lashing they received from the Vatican." Father Alejandro took some deep breaths. "I've also been recently dealing with a personal issue."

Reflecting on the previous evening, Father Tomassi wondered when — and if — Alejandro was going to come clean about what transpired. "Was that what happened last night?"

"Sort of. I'm losing my hearing."

Tomassi couldn't tell what collapsing in the bathroom had to do with hearing. "Old age? Underlying condition?"

"Funny you should ask. I've always been hard of hearing. Lost much of it when I was a child. Severe ear infections. Scarred up everything pretty good."

"Wow. Could never guess. Seem to be doing well with me now. Did fine earlier during mass. Unless, of course, you're wearing some kind of hearing device. You're in your fifties, aren't you?"

"Fifty-one."

"Ahh. We're in the same age bracket, though I'm at the other end."

"In our line of work, it is so vital to be engaged. Focused, as you know. I've learned to read lips and adjust my surroundings to pick up what I need. There are also times where I swear that it comes and goes. When I was a child, though... those days were much more difficult."

"I can imagine."

"Ears would pop at the most inconvenient times. Then I couldn't hear anything. When people would speak low, they might as well have been whispering. I couldn't hear anything. Hated libraries because everyone would speak so quietly in there."

"Yeah, three years shy of sixty and I feel myself getting there. Can't imagine what it must have been like going through that as a child."

Father Alejandro turned to look at Father Tomassi. "But in prayer, that silence is like... it's like a force-field. A protective bubble. Nothing can get through. If prayer is about being intentional, it's the best way to show respect. I think it's attributed to my success as an exorcist." His smile faded. "Just recently, out of the blue, though, my hearing became progressively worse."

"I guess it's bound to happen. Between age and what you do. It can't be good on the body."

"It isn't. It's devastating on several levels: physically. Mentally. Emotionally. Spiritually. But the hearing situation has become incredibly problematic."

"And you're dealing with this how?"

"Was getting pretty desperate. Then I happened upon this new hearing device."

"Interesting."

"I don't know. How I came about the business and the technology just seems... too convenient. Too coincidental not to be suspicious."

"You don't think it's the Lord speaking to you in some way?"

"Far from it."

"Oh?"

"This is technology I've never seen before. It's a device that I can wear completely in the canal."

"All the way in?"

"All the way in. Hidden."

"Is it made in another country?"

"I think that's what they've led me to believe."

"And it works being so far inside the canal? If that's the case, it sounds like a marvelous invention."

"It is but I am hearing strange things, David. Scary stuff. I can hear demons. Voices of evil walking the earth. Some aware of what they are doing. Some oblivious to where they are."

Tomassi couldn't help but smile. "Please

don't be cross. It just seems natural that you would hear stuff you normally wouldn't when using the new technology. I mean all the way in the ear. The body is probably making noises that you're picking up. Makes sense now that a whole new world is open to you."

"It's something. This new tech. I'll give you that. Nice not having to walk around with a box hung around my neck or having some large clam shell over the back of my ear. It will be exciting to see what tech is on the horizon in these years leading up to 2000. I mean we're what sixteen or seventeen years out. When I think of the possibilities, I am always transported back to the Seattle World's Fair with their World of Tomorrow theme."

"That was back in '62, right?"

"Yeah. April of 1962."

"Well, judging by the space shuttles and computers, I fear in twenty years men our age won't even be able to comprehend what the world is like."

"If it's anything like these little buggers, you may be right."

The men paused to watch a vehicle make its way around from the main parking lot to the back exit. At first Tomassi thought the sisters had a visitor. He looked to Father Alejandro. "Have you discussed any of your concerns with your audiologist?"

"He's been rather coy. I don't know. Maybe it's just me. I have two more weeks before I need to return the devices for a refund if I choose not to keep them. They aren't even charging me much. Gave me a steep discount once they found out I was," and he paused to make air quotes, "a 'man of the cloth'."

"So, what's the problem?"

"I'm not comfortable with what I hear when I wear them. And I'm not comfortable being indebted to this center. I can't explain it."

"Have you worn them in public yet? In crowds? Is this happening when you're alone?"

"Oh, yes, I've worn them in public."

"And?"

"When it first happened, I thought someone was playing a prank on me. David, this is happening when I am alone. In public. It doesn't matter. It happened last night in the rectory when you found me."

Tomassi shook his head. "This may sound James Bondish and all but there's no receiver of some kind on the device?"

"None that I or anyone else can tell."

"So what about the business? You're not comfortable with the center or the owners?"

"The audiologist owns the business with his wife. I've seen some stuff that matches the Red Flag vibe I get when I am around them. Makes my blood run cold."

"I see."

"Much too welcoming, if that makes any sense. Too good to be true kind of stuff, you know. Saying all the right things. Almost reading your mind kind of thing. Huggy. Weepy. Talking about things that go beyond the scope of the average service. Sales pitch stories that are just too well choreographed. Mind you, these are hearing devices. Slick, David. Very slick." There was a change in Alejandro's voice. "There's something else, too. Something I've never witnessed outside of an exorcism."

"What is it?"

Father Alejandro shuddered. "Tar black pits for eye sockets."

"EBO? You're certain?"

"My lips to God's ears. Yes. Evil Black Oculi. I am sure of it. Saw it with my own eyes. That's when I knew. It wasn't just a feeling at that point. *IT* brazenly revealed itself to me."

"What's the name of the place?"

"Hear More. Hear More Hearing Center. The audiologist and his wife regularly run these workshops to bring people in. Nothing advertised you see. It's all by word-of-mouth. Then they have a vetting session before the invite."

Tomassi made a face. "How odd. To whom are they catering?"

"Specifically those with hearing loss of course. After all, it's life changing, right? But they are also luring inexperienced entrepreneurs looking to become franchise owners. But it's the damnedest thing. They run it almost like a cult. Get this: Because I questioned them about the devices and the need for these workshops I'm obligated to attend, they've been acting as if I offended them in some way. As if I don't appreciate them enough."

"But you paid for them?"

"Yes."

"And now the voices."

"Voices of evil spirits, I tell you."

"You don't see them?"

"Aside from the black eyes of the owners, no. I just hear them."

"Do you hear them without the devices?"

"No. Thankfully. But make no mistake, these devices are evil. Whether they, themselves —"

"The owners?"

"Yes, Don and Mara Abaddon... Whether they are evil or they've been corrupted... possessed... I can't say. The demonic infestation through the devices is surely an extension of what surrounds them."

"Makes sense."

"But I also think the spirits... Because of my work, I think they've been tipped off. Like there's a different energy or connection because they are aware that I possess this newfound ability."

"Are they specifically speaking to you?"

"They weren't initially. But as they've become aware that I can hear them, they've begun to do just that."

"What are they saying?"

"Vile things, David. Creepy. Filthy. Blasphemous things. Then there are the threats." Father Alejandro looked over at his counterpart. "They keep encouraging me to kill myself."

"Are you suicidal?"

"Not at all."

"Were you ever?"

"No."

"Then that's a good sign, is it not? It means they fear you, Alex. They fear what you can hear. I would argue they fear what you can do, too."

"I agree. To a certain extent. But lately things seem to indicate something big is on the horizon."

"Big?"

"I'm thinking in the form of a possession. A job. An exorcism against a malevolent evil. I've gotten some indicators in the past. Nothing like this, though."

"You know this to be true?"

Father Alejandro looked out over the field the students use during recess and gym. Looked at the trees that were partially bare. "I feel it. Everything around me confirms it. Dreams. The way they speak. Day visions even."

Tomassi noticed Alejandro quivering as he flashed a troubling look. "You're afraid."

Alejandro swallowed hard as he recalled the demon posing as his mother the previous evening calling out to him. "I know you went through something a few years ago yourself. That's why you're not shocked by what I've shared. You're guarded about it. But it's in your eyes. You don't speak of it." Father Alejandro studied the elder priest's face. "You know more than you let on about the events at the hospital that Easter. You're a good man, David Tomassi. Yes, I am afraid. But I feel goodness when I am around you. I feel God. I trust you."

"I'm here for whatever you need. I am sorry that I am not an exorcist, though."

"Letting me share service this morning. Sitting here with me now. Your patience and understanding last evening. These give me strength. And comfort. Uplifts my spirit."

"What about the Vatican? Is there any way they can help? Anyone you can talk to?"

"None that I trust."

"What do you plan to do next?"

"Returning the devices is the first step. I also have an ask."

"You want me to accompany you when you meet with them?"

"How did you guess?"

"Strength in numbers to send a message to all things evil."

Walking back to the car, Joseph probed Father Tomassi for answers to his lingering questions. He carried two of the three boxes from Father Alejandro's room, fighting to disregard the ringing that started in his ears moments before they walked outside. "So, Alex is in Florida. Bumps into these two peddling this new hearing technology. A few weeks later they hand deliver the devices to him here in Connecticut."

"That's what he said."

"And then they got cross with him over his not wanting to keep them."

"Seems so. And for his lack of fealty."

"And now he's dead."

"Well, officially Father Alex suffered a myocardial infarction while overseas during a prayer service."

"Unofficially?"

"He was overtaken by the Demonic Triumverate during a very intense exorcism."

Joseph placed the boxes he was carrying on the trunk of the car while waiting for Tomassi to catch up and unlock the vehicle. Waving off a group of flies he tried to ignore the growing hum in his head. "You didn't exactly believe him at first, did you? Even with all we've been through."

"I think there are some things I don't want to… still don't want to… believe. Or accept." After placing Alejandro's personal effects box he was carrying in the back seat, Tomassi climbed behind the wheel. "Father Alex's situation proved once more we're up against not just supernatural evil. We're up against human evil. An evil that is operating blatantly in front of us. Nearly mocking us at every turn."

"How can we expect to make any progress if we continue to lose so many of our own on the battlefield?" Joseph asked slipping into the passenger side as Tomassi turned over the ignition and backed out of the parking space.

Tomassi was resolute. "I believe, despite how it looks, we are not alone. Not just in spirit either. The people we need to help us fight the coming evil just haven't found us yet. In the meantime, we will mourn our brother but also honor him. And since the Abaddons are supposed to be in state this coming week—"

"You're clear," Joseph said before Tomassi pulled out onto the busy highway.

"We'll look into this Hear More Hearing Center."

"That may not be possible." Joseph uncurling the fingers of his right hand to reveal Father Alejandro's hearing aids in his palm.

Father Tomassi turned to ask his friend what he meant just as a horn blaring semi slammed into the 1980 Chevy Malibu.

KEYNOTE

The tall handsome young man thanked the young girl at the door after learning his table would be ready in a few minutes by gently squeezing her arm and flashing a gleaming smile. Dressed in matching slacks and blazer, he wore a collared white polo shirt with its top buttons undone.

Strolling over to the bar area, he leaned onto the thick mahogany counter and ordered a mimosa. Once more flashing that smile of his, he was flirtatious and confident with the female bartender. This helped him get served immediately even though the area was crowded. The thick wad of bills he removed from his pocket held together with a gold-plated dollar sign clip was also quite the attention-getter.

The man checked his watch, a Rolex with a large face. It was very masculine and matched the pinky ring he wore on his right hand. He was waiting on his date. A successful young lady of her own, she was more a friend with benefits than a date. The two had a deal that when they weren't exclusive with anyone, they would accompany each other to events so as not to arrive alone. Projecting the right image was everything for business. That's when he saw an average looking woman approach a little man seated at one of the high cocktail tables in the corner nearby. He couldn't get over the other man's legs dangling so far above the floor.

"Hi, you must be Madge," the man at the bar overheard the seated man say.

"Logan, right?" the woman asked as the man slid off the stool to stand beside her.

"How'd you guess?" he asked making light of a glaring attribute his date wasn't sure how to respond to. "Our table is almost ready. Everything okay?"

"Just nervous." She was suddenly self-conscious feeling the hotel's bar area patrons' eyes on her. She wasn't prepared to spend an afternoon with a man who only came up to her breasts. Her greatest fear was someone taking a photo of her and posting it to an AOL, MySpace, or Internet forum.

"I understand. In-person sessions can be awkward. But after this morning's presentation I have a nice afternoon planned. There's an art show we can access via the ferry. It's an annual event they have here in Port Jefferson. Goes on all weekend as a matter of fact."

"I don't know," she replied. She was kneading her hands spending more time looking around the room than looking at Logan.

"Would you like to sit down?"

"No. I'm good for the moment."

"Okay, so maybe if you're not up for an entire afternoon. We can just do lunch then. Or a drink."

"Will you excuse me?"

"Of course. I'll get us something to drink in the meantime."

Logan approached the crowded bar, navigating elbows and people carrying drinks who weren't expecting someone so short in the crowd. Their expressions were akin to that of bumping into a child — amused before becoming perplexed given the setting. Then abject horror that it was actually a tiny version of an adult male. Once at the bar, Logan was grateful for an alert and observant bartender who took his order right away without having to madly gesticulate in order to get someone's attention. Logan made sure to tip him well.

Heading back to the table with a mimosa and a coffee in hand Logan had to continually speak up with "Excuse me" and "Coming through," lest an errant elbow or hind end bump into him or the drinks. It was clear once he reached Madge, however, things were not going to go as planned. She had returned but still wasn't sitting at the very high chic cocktail table. With her already appearing uncomfortable, it didn't make sense for him to stand for much longer seeing how the contrast in height only drew unwanted attention. As it was, he was the same height as the stool. Perhaps sitting would make her more comfortable since he could look her in the eyes.

Glancing over the crowded room, he would have chosen a more appropriate place to sit but there weren't any other tables. Wouldn't be for a while, he gathered, since there was a big event going on at the hotel. Probably not the only one either.

"I'm not sure this is going to work out," Madge said breaking the awkward silence.

"Okay." Logan tried offering her a choice of beverage. "Mimosa or coffee?"

Madge leaned over, her hand flat against her chest to keep her top from opening. "I can't hear you."

"I just asked if you—"

"Look, I'm sorry. I didn't know."

"Didn't know what?"

"That you were so…"

"Short?"

"Short," she repeated without hearing what he said.

Logan smirked. "Yeah. I am sensing that. It's bit of a shock to some people."

"I'm sure you're very nice and all."

"Keep in mind the conversations we've had. Today is really about getting you out and about again."

"I really can't hear you all that well and I don't want to have to keep bending over. It's just that I expected we'd be able to talk face-to-face. You know, eye-to-eye."

He noted her last line. And understood. "You're uncomfortable. I get it."

"I am. *Very* to tell you the truth. I'm sorry but I have to go."

As the woman exited, the tall man at the bar sauntered over to Logan's table. He loitered long enough for Logan to hop back up on to the stool before he spoke. "Tough break there, huh?"

"I'm sorry?"

"Saw what happened with your girl." He then grimaced and clicked his tongue. "Ouch. Tough break."

"Oh." Slightly embarrassed, the man at the table chuckled. "It's nothing."

"Must go through that a lot."

"Not so much. Not as much as you might imagine."

"Really? Well, I don't know how you do it. Then again, I don't know how half the people in here do it. Overweight. Unattractive. Boring. Unmotivated." He gently swished his glass to mix the orange juice and champagne. "What'd you order?" the man asked pointing at the glass filled with a pink liquid.

"It's a mimosa. Same as what you're having, I gather." Upon the man's puzzled look, Logan clarified his response. "Grapefruit mimosa."

"No kidding. Never had one before."

"Be my guest. There's coffee there too if you want it."

"So, uh, no offense there, bud, but no one takes a man your height seriously. Just as no one gives a girl the time of day if she's fugly. Or fat. Doesn't matter if it's business or relationships. I mean, hey, just look at the presidential statistics."

"Do tell. How do you mean?"

"The taller candidates have always been voted in."

"Always?"

"Most. Statistically speaking. And they aren't even that short. I mean, not your kind of short. That's how much it means to be a man... a man's man is a man of a certain height."

"Interesting," Logan replied amused. "I should write that down somewhere."

"Yes, you should," the other said with a wink and click of the tongue.

"Are you a religious person?"

"Nah. Don't believe in much of that hooey."

Logan smiled. He wasn't surprised. "Some call it religion. Others refer to it as spirituality. But the universe has a way of making things right, you know. Maybe even teaching us a few lessons along the way."

"Okay..."

"You see, each individual has more power than they realize, regardless of gender, weight, color, socioeconomics... even *height*. I could go on. Let me just underscore that people need to believe in themselves and the universe will find a way to make things work."

"You keep telling yourself that."

"It doesn't discount the need to work hard. But recognizing one's gifts is integral to success. Like yourself, I'm sure."

"Whatever you say, Oprah. I mean, yeah, I work hard. Play hard too. But I'm also prime rib compared to the cubed steak that's in here. So, was it a blinder?"

"A what?"

"With the vadge who walked out on you. Was it a blind date?"

"Wait. What did you just call her? Her name is Madge."

The taller man smiled as he downed the rest of his mimosa eyeing a grinning waitress with deep dimples.

Shaking his head, Logan found himself uncomfortable with this cocksure man who seemingly had no filter. "That's just rude. As for the date, no, it wasn't a blind date. Well, yes. In a sense. We've only been talking on the phone."

"Ahh. So you didn't tell her then."

"Tell her what exactly?"

"That you're a midget." He then clinked the glass of grapefruit mimosa against the cup of coffee. "Cheers."

"Should I have also announced that I am black, too?"

The man nearly spit out his mimosa. "You are?"

"Yes. Partially. Even if I don't look it. And I'm not a midget."

"Damn! This stuff is really good," the man commented after another sip of Logan's mimosa. Then he returned to the topic at hand. "Not a midget or you don't identify as a midget?"

"I am NOT a midget."

"All right. All right. Jeez. Don't get all worked up. But, Dude, you come up to my freakin' knees. Never been around a guy so short. We should take a photo together. No one is going to believe me."

"You're exaggerating now. It's more like your waist. And I'm not upset. You're very vulgar and your terminology is inaccurate."

"Whatever. I've gotta admit, though, I'd be buying *you* a drink right about now if I were gay." The man put out his hand. "Maxwell Short. Friends call me Max."

"This is exactly what I am talking about," the shorter man said as he reluctantly shook the other's hand. "Interesting last name."

"I know, right! Here I am nearly nine feet tall and you're what now?"

"Nine feet, huh? Now you're really exaggerating. Anyway, my name is—"

"Logan. I know. I overheard you two. So, what are you, then, if you aren't a midget?"

Logan glanced around the room to see if he was being punked before he answered. "I am actually a dwarf."

"Is that where they got the Snow White story from? Hey, now! Wait. Wait." He put the champagne flute down so he could be broad and physical with his gestures. "I have another. Sure you're not really a live cabbage patch doll? A real live Weeble Wobble?" The man clapped his hands and howled with laughter. "Sorry. Sometimes I crack myself up."

"Are you finished?" Logan waited for Max to compose himself. "For future reference, if you're under five feet you are considered a dwarf. Those under three feet are midgets."

Max swallowed the rest of the grapefruit mimosa. "Dude, my housecleaner's got an old relative from Italy that is just below five feet and she does not look like... like *you* people."

"Us people?"

"You know. Like Oompa Loompas."

Logan pursed his lips and exhaled disapprovingly through his nose. "My goodness, can you be any more offensive?"

"Lighten up, there, Tiny. What? Can't take a joke?"

"It's not even the Oompa Loompa comment. You've been incredibly crass the entire conversation."

"Pssht. No one else seems to mind. My clients don't mind. So long as they get the best deals. And that's what Max does."

"So what you were referring to is a form of dwarfism. Of which there are over 200 different kinds."

"Whatever, man. Don't care. Just playing with you," Max said as he rustled the diminutive man's hair.

Logan swatted Max's hand away nearly knocking over the empty flute. "Seriously? How old are you?" Their actions drew a few looks.

Just then a very tall, slim, attractive woman approached the table.

Max adjusted his crotch before elbowing Logan. "See. Now that's a woman. You could have done a lot better. If you were taller, that is."

Once at the table she looked at Max. "Are you ready?" she asked. Tense. Annoyed.

"Just waiting on our table," he said putting his arm around her to draw her close. His attempt to kiss her on the lips was thwarted when she turned her head.

"I know I just came from there. Jesus, Max. You need a breath mint. Let's go. They are ready to seat us."

"Fantastic. Kiera, this is..." Max snapped his fingers in an attempt to recall the shorter man's name.

"Logan."

"Right." He winked and pointed at Logan. "This here's Logan. Almost had it. It was on the tip of my tongue."

Kiera, however, couldn't be bothered. "I don't really..." she began with an eye roll before saying hello but without looking at Logan. "Can we go now?" she asked as she began walking away from the table. It wasn't so much a question as a command.

"I thought we could invite him to sit with us," Max said within earshot. "He seems interesting."

"I'd rather not. And interesting why? That's not a man. Besides I don't like standing next to people who only come up to my ass. It makes me uncomfortable."

The man laughed and elbowed the girl. "I know, right. Still, it's kinda hot!" He then turned to say something to Logan, but Logan spoke first.

"You better hurry or she might leave without you."

"Right. Damn."

"Hey, Max!"

Max was on his way to catch up with Kiera. "Yo! What?"

Elbows on the table, Logan was resting his chin on clasped hands. "I'm sorry. I just had to ask you something."

"Okay, what? Make it quick."

"Are you happy?"

"What kind of question is that?" he asked more focused on his escort than Logan. She was about to disappear into the banquet room.

"It's simple enough. Are you happy?"

"With her?"

"Sure. Her. And life. Who you are. All of it."

Max seemed offended. "Seriously? You called me back over for that? What? You think you're better than me?"

"I did not say that, nor did I imply that."

"Dude, I'm a hell of lot happier than you. I'm successful. Gotta bangin' bachelor pad. Good business with steady clients. Have access to anything I want. Can pretty much get any smokin' hot girl I want. You won't find me stuck in crowds sniffing crotches all the time."

Logan raised his eyebrows.

"What?"

"You. That's what you think I do all the time? Sniff crotches."

"You know what I mean. Once again, you're getting all offended. Peace out, little man." Max then left to catch up with Kiera.

"Hot damn," the man in the gray slacks exclaimed as he unzipped himself and moved in close to the urinal. "Saw you talking to that little guy earlier. Little squirt comes up to my balls."

"Dude, I bet the girls love it," Max replied from two urinals over. The two men were seated at the same table in the nearby event room, but Max had already forgotten his name. It was a vice of his and it happened a lot with his clients if he didn't make a point to get their business cards or write anything down.

"Probably the only time I'd want to be that short. No dropping coins. Fit under the table."

"Under the dress," Max added laughing.

"Right! Oh, man!"

"And imagine dating a fat girl?"

"That's some weekend warrior shit right there."

"You're not kidding."

Mr. Gray Slacks leaned his head back and uttered a guttural sigh of relief. "I've had to piss like a racehorse for the longest time."

"Too much coffee?"

"Too many mimosas," he replied as they both laughed.

"Perfect time, too. You know, before the speaker goes on. Besides, this is the first time I have someone from work accompanying me to one of these things and... well, you heard her. She won't shut up." He stopped talking for a moment to complete his business. "Jesus, can you imagine him using the urinal?"

"Who? The little guy?"

"Might as well use the urinal to wash his face."

Max snickered. "Probably plops his chin right on it."

"Actually, that would be why we use the toilets," Logan announced as he exited the handicap stall behind them. "And even then some short statured people can't reach or comfortably relieve themselves. Something, huh? All that trouble for a basic need."

"Oh, crap," the gray slacks man said sarcastically. "Looks like we're in trouble now."

"Just think about what I said, gentlemen," the shorter one remarked as he washed his hands. "Think about how you'd feel if that was your dad, your uncle, or your grandfather. How demeaning it would be. Emasculating even." He then exited ahead of the taller guys.

Max and the man in gray slacks looked at each other before bursting out in uproarious laughter.

"Uh, hello. Good afternoon. Good afternoon, everyone. I trust you all had a safe trip in. I know some arrived last night and some came in just this morning. The Expo, if you haven't ventured through it yet, is on the other side of the hotel in the other banquet room. As a reminder, we also have a silent auction taking place. There are some freebies there as well, so please check that out. Now, how about that wonderful brunch!"

The room erupted in applause.

"The hotel and their staff have been amazing. By now most of you have had your tables cleared. Coffee and tea will be coming around for you to enjoy during the keynote. Then we have workshops based on what you signed up for starting at two. For those of you interested in this evening's mixer, it will be held just outside here where many of you were waiting for the tables to become available.

"Now we do have one change. Our original keynote speaker couldn't make it today on account of a family emergency." There was a sea of audible groans as many of them had traveled to specifically hear the scheduled author and speaker. "Well, now, fear not. It's not a wasted trip. We have someone who was gracious enough to drop everything and fly out here. While he won't be joining us for the weekend, he has agreed to be here this morning with us.

"A Master Certified Coach and speaker himself, he too is an author. His latest, *In Their Shoes*, is currently a sixteen-week *New York Times* bestseller. He's here to share how we might best interact with others — be they clients, patients, students — by essentially putting ourselves in their shoes.

"Now, without further ado, please give a warm welcome to Logan Grant."

"No way," the gray slacks guy said across the table from Max over a smattering of applause.

Kiera leaned into Max. "Isn't that the man you were talking to earlier?"

"Yeah. I'll be damned. It really is him. We ran into him in the bathroom too."

The stage was a set piece in the largest of the hotel's banquet halls. Leading up to the stage were high steps that Logan had to carefully navigate without tripping or falling in front of a crowd of about two hundred. But he was used to it. It was once he reached the podium that he realized his height was overlooked. Even though he made sure to initiate a request before flying out, as is often the case, it wasn't a priority for the hotel. There was no stool or step nearby. Because of this, only his forehead was visible to the crowd gathered for the opening address.

Logan heard the chuckles in the room as they all waited expectantly for what was next.

The loudest of the laughs came from Max's table, which happened to be near the stage.

"Gotta love this guy," he said for those at the table to hear. Then he spoke up louder for Logan's benefit. "Looks like you may have come up a bit short there, little buddy."

There were some guffaws in response to Max's outburst. Mostly uncomfortable chuckles. The woman accompanying Gray Slacks Man slapped him for laughing before shooting Max a dirty look. Kiera's eyes were focused on the podium. The other couple at the table, two guys, faced the stage and had their backs to everyone else. They were whispering and nodding.

Then came the microphone feedback as Logan removed the wired mic from the stand and rounded the podium to begin his delivery.

Logan laughed as he was met with a round of applause. "I haven't even started yet. Thank you. Thank you. Very kind of you. Sorry about the feedback a moment ago." He gestured to the podium. "Sometimes these things happen. Right? It's a fact of life.

"The reality is this: Life is full of awkward moments. As I tell my wife, it's a part of being human. It's all part of the human experience.

"Why just this morning, I was attempting to walk a client through reestablishing her footing." Logan glanced over at Max for a moment before continuing. "A bit of an introvert, she had been hurt in a relationship and further isolated herself. She's taken some baby steps, but this morning was the biggest yet. One she was willing to take.

But she discovered it will take some additional time to get over the awkwardness she feels re-acclimating herself. And that is okay.

"People often ask where I get my patience from. It's because I put myself in the shoes of my clients and those with whom I meet. If we want to truly be successful in all we do, especially the many relationships we have, we need to consider not taking so many things for granted. That what comes easy to you may not for someone else and vice versa. And that each of us, like our experiences, is unique.

"That is why I am asking you to consider today, this weekend, while you are in your workshops and when you return to your businesses, consider what it is like to be in the shoes of those around you. It will redefine your approach to so many things and bring about an organic shift to your language and authenticity to your actions."

While speaking, Logan moved from one end of the stage area to the other. This way he was able to address the entire room. Just as he was about to delve deeper into his topic, his lips were moving but there was no sound.

The crowd groaned as Logan tapped the dead microphone. Then they applauded him again as he responded positively to the situation. With a genuine smile, he appeared unaffected. Adept at such moments, he simply placed the mic on the floor of the stage and continued by naturally projecting his voice.

Max was up out of his seat determined to remedy the situation while hotel personnel scrambled to find another mic off stage. "I got you, little man," he yelled eagerly and confidently. "I got this. No need to shorten your speech."

Logan held up a hand as he spoke and shook his head at Max. His new friend, however, refused to heed the warning. He began fiddling with the mic's plug, pulling it from the jack and then inserting it back into the aged amp.

The second time Max did this, there were some sparks. But he ignored them. The third time there was a flash of light accompanied by a loud pop as Max was blown back several feet.

Maxwell awoke to a nurse shining a light into his eyes. Spreading the lids of the left eye and then the right eye open, she was using her pen light to register each pupil's response. "Good evening, Mr. Short. How do you feel?"

"Somebody better call God and let him know he's missing an angel."

"Do you remember what happened?" the nurse asked ignoring her patient's flirtatiousness. "Guess you gave everyone quite the scare."

Though he was feeling a bit disoriented, he was immediately smitten with the nurse tending to him. Her hands smelled like perfumed moisturizer and there was a mix of coffee and spearmint on her warm breath. "I was at a hotel. I remember that much."

"Anything after that?"

"Pink mimosas." Then he smiled. "They are very tasty."

"Nothing else?" she asked suddenly aware of his wandering eyes.

"Not really."

"Well, you were electrocuted. Suffered a shock from sound stage equipment I am told. Guess the hotel went dark for hours thanks to you."

"Really? Guess my mom was right, then."

"About?"

"I really do have an electric personality."

"You'll notice your right hand is bandaged. It's nothing serious," the nurse noted, still impervious to Max's charms.

"C'mon. That was a good one. Not even a smile?"

"Consider yourself lucky, Mr. Short. You could have died. Guess the universe isn't done with you yet. Anyway, the doctor will be here momentarily to check on you and explain everything."

Movement in the hall caught Max's attention.

The nurse smiled, happy he finally noticed they were there. "We'll let them in shortly. The doctor wishes to talk to you first."

"My mouth is dry. Could I have some water?"

"Of course." The nurse rolled the tray closer so Max could have better access to the cup later. Grabbing the cup on the tray she poured in ice water from the brightly pastel-colored plastic water pitcher. Leaning into the prone patient, the nurse brought the cup's straw to his lips.

"Those people out there. Who are they? What's going on?" he asked after a few refreshing sips, his eyes continuing to peek where they shouldn't.

"It's your wife and family, Mr. Short. So you might want to stop being a perv trying to look down my scrub top."

Max giggled before closing his eyes. He knew she liked it. She was only being hard to get. Then what she said struck him. *Wife?* That couldn't be right. He wasn't married.

"The doctor's here to see you now," the nurse announced as she exited the room.

"Doc, you're not going to believe the dream I had." Max opened his eyes when he felt the doctor place fingers on his wrist to check his pulse. "Wait. You?"

"Yep, it's me. Logan," the doctor said in between looking at his watch and doing calculations in his head. "Hiya, Max!"

"But you're so... tall."

Dr. Logan revealed a toothy grin. "I know. I know. All my patients give me a hard time about it, especially the shorter ones." He then pulled a pen light from his white coat to check Max's pupils. "Looking good, Max. Looking good."

"Short patients? But I'm not short."

Dr. Logan chuckled. "Let me guess. You're about to tell me you identify with tall people, right?" He then reached for the spring-loaded aluminum clipboard containing Max's patient logs. "Nice. Okay. Vitals are good. Now, I don't know how your family will feel with you being in denial and all," the doctor said with a wink. "But they will certainly be happy to see you."

"Who?"

"Your family, Max," the doctor said removing the stethoscope from his neck. He placed the ear tips to his ears and positioned the chestpiece between the second and third finger of his left hand. "From what I've been told, they've been standing outside this room since they heard you were awake." Placing the larger part of the chestpiece over Max's chest, he listened carefully to his patient's heart.

Max looked at the large floating heads moving in the hall. Aside from the heads, they looked like children. They were so short only from the neck up was visible above the solid bottom half of the partitioned wall. "Wow. I mean bravo. Brah-vo! Hell of a joke. That's good."

"What is?"

"The next thing you're going to tell me is that I'm also a mid—that I'm also short."

"I guess it's how you feel that defines you." Dr. Logan returned the stethoscope to lay around his neck. "Okay, just one more request. Would you mind wiggling your toes for me, please?"

Max looked down at his body as the doctor pulled aside the blanket.

"Hey, fantastic job," Dr. Logan noted. "You seemed a bit dazed and confused but that should clear up shortly. Shall I let them in?"

"It can't be," Max uttered shaking with fury.

The doctor motioned for the family to enter. "What's that?"

"I'm a… I'm a… I'm a freak!"

"Hardly. You're a healthy little person," Logan said crossing his arms.

"I'm a midget," Max seethed.

Logan shook his head. "You mean to tell me you already forgot?"

"Forgot what?"

There was an amused look on Logan's face. "This morning. Under five feet is a dwarf. A midget is under three feet."

The family of little people entered the room headed for the bed.

"You did this to me," Max fumed between clenched teeth. "I don't know how you did this, but I swear to God—"

"You mean I provided you with a happy family that loves you so you could gain some much-needed perspective." The doctor then turned to the incoming individuals. "Good evening, everyone. Max, I'm happy to report, is improving," he declared. "We will be keeping him overnight for observation, however. So get in there and spend some quality time with him."

"Logan!" Max yelled.

"Oops, I almost forgot. Excuse me." The doctor maneuvered around some of the family members already bedside so he could lean into Max to whisper in his ear. "Guess you should be careful about who you make fun of in the future."

"You son of a bitch. Who are you?"

Logan patted Max on the head before tussling his tightly curled head of hair. "He's going to be okay everyone. Just getting over a little disorientation."

Max furiously slapped aside Logan's hand. "How long do I have to stay like this?"

"However long it takes," Logan replied as he interacted with the family before turning to leave.

"Where are you going? You need to fix this, Logan. You hear me. You need to fix this."

"You weren't listening earlier," Logan replied with a wave and without turning around. "It's not me. I didn't do this. It's the universe."

As the doctor exited the room, Max spotted a horrified and bewildered Kiera staring at him through the window.

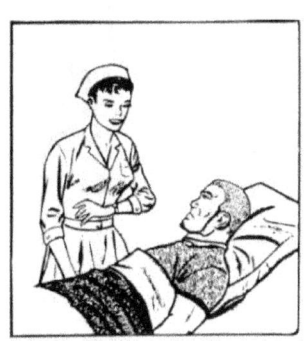

ABOUT THE AUTHOR

There's nothing like things that go bump in the night to get the heart racing. Who doesn't like a good scare?

As a youngster, Ray LeCara Jr found himself buried in collections of short spooky stories by Stephen King, Peter Straub, and Clive Barker.

In this collection of short stories, LeCara celebrates the genre with five haunting tales.

A former public school teacher, LeCara now teaches students worldwide online and, in addition to writing, can be found life coaching and working in local independent films.

OTHER BOOKS
BY THIS AUTHOR

Future Destiny

When Worlds Collide

The Forgotten Prophecy

*Of Space & Time: A
Collection of Short Sci-Fi Stories*

*From Where I Sit: A
Collection of Short Fiction*